FOG

The Jeffrey Stories

by
Christopher Brookhouse

Grateful acknowledgment is made to *The Sewanee Review* to reprint "Changing Light," to *Confrontation* to reprint "Shot," to *The Gettysburg Review* to reprint "Naked."

Copyright 2004

All rights reserved. No portion of this book may be reproduced in any form by any means electronic or mechanical, including information storage and retrieval systems, without permission in writing from Safe Harbor Books, with the exception of passages quoted in reviews.

FOG
is a work of fiction.
Any resemblance of its characters to people living or dead
is unintended and coincidental.

First Edition

ISBN 0-9665798-6-0
Library of Congress Card Number: 200309595

Designed by Dean Bornstein
Jacket design by Amy Lynn Plourde

For
Ann Page Stecker
a most generous and uncommon reader

CONTENTS

Shot / 1

Milly / 14

Privacy / 57

C Words / 65

Changing Light / 86

Bones / 96

Naked / 128

The Apologist / 151

The Man Who Kissed ZaSu Pitts / 162

Sooty / 176

Fog / 185

Car Talk / 239

Yes / 248

Be You / 265

~ SHOT ~

Summer. The Volvos from Massachusetts fill the town again.

My name is Rudy. I find people rentals on the lake. I like the commissions, of course. I like the bodies more, the tanned legs in shorts. I don't mean the college girls, but the women turned forty who keep in shape and know they look good. They're spoken for, but they enjoy being seen, admired. I do a lot of that these days. I'm forty-three. Living practically in Canada and barely two months of good weather a year dulled my wife's enthusiasm for New Hampshire. She moved to Texas. We're divorced. The permanent population of Jeffrey, New Hampshire, is eleven hundred. The average age is over sixty.

Out of the corner of my eye I see brown legs ascending the steps of the inn. I turn to appraise, to dream. I focus on the road again, just in time. The squeal drifts away. The smell of scorched tread lingers. The woman in the crosswalk glares at me. I say sorry. She can't hear me. She doesn't move. She looks at me, looks toward the inn. Then so quickly, so gracefully, so nonchalantly that when she puts down her skirt I would swear she hadn't done it, the woman raises her skirt, shows me all her legs, and more. Then she strides to the sidewalk, shaking her head, her hand rearranging her hair across her shoulder.

The rest of the afternoon I can't clear my mind. At six o'clock I'm into my second Johnny Walker, sitting at the bar at the inn, recounting the event to Jimmy while he mixes drinks for the dinner crowd in the other room. So what color underwear was she wearing? he asks.

Jimmy acts skeptical when I mention mine was the only car at the crosswalk. Main Street is usually busy at two in the afternoon. A beautiful afternoon. Everyone was at the lake, I suggest. Jimmy smirks, his expression for I'm having trouble believing this, and pours a Manhattan.

Not white. Something dark.

The smirk again. You sure she was wearing any?

I shrug, like the question doesn't have resonance. Truth is, when I was driving away I didn't think she was.

That detail was the beginning. The first detail to start the scene replaying all afternoon. Sometimes at the supermarket a lady bends over to feel the produce and I glimpse her breast. Or a woman sliding out of her car reveals a little more than she meant to. Moments to quicken the heart, images that don't stick in the mind very long. I smile and forget them. I don't forget a woman lifting her skirt on Main Street at two o'clock on Wednesday afternoon.

Another? Jimmy asks.

I shake my head. In the mirror behind Jimmy I see the trophy bass caught and stuffed in 1960. Two large mouths. I'm alive in my watering hole. It isn't. I'm extra careful driving home.

A couple of messages. One of my clients doesn't like a painting. Swears it wasn't there when I showed her the house. She would remember such a picture. Can she take it down? Another can't get his ice maker to work. I open my own refrigerator and drop a handful of cubes into my glass before I add Mr. Walker. I live near the woods. While I stand at the stove making pasta, I see a moose by the trees at the end of the yard. It wanders off toward the pond across the street. Sometimes a bear will show up and shake the seed out of the bird feeder.

I finish supper, clean the dishes, watch a few innings on the sports channel, then take a book to bed, the town history published in 1951, the 150th anniversary of Jeffrey's founding. My thoughts skip from the Red Sox to the '38 hurricane. I fall asleep. I don't think of the woman again until she wakes me in the dark. The underwear question. The mind takes poor snapshots. I keep going over them as I drift in and out of sleep. I'm not happy with myself. The words *adolescent* and *prurient* apply. If my clients could see inside my head, I'd be poor forever.

In the morning I try to be objective, clinical. Doctor, I'm attracted to women. Let's be candid. Lately their favors have been out of reach. Naturally a woman showing herself to me is disturbing.

Naturally, my boy. I understand.

Thank you, Doctor. So why did she do that?

Yes, my boy, that is the question. The underwear business is irrelevant. What's your theory?

Well, she was angry. I could have killed her. She saw I was paying attention to a woman's legs instead of where I was driving. If I wanted to look at a pair of legs, she'd show me hers. She was thinking, Mine are ten times better; one look and you'll know. And one look is all you get. Ever.

My boy, I think you understand perfectly.

Off to work I go. Morning light on the lake. The client is oiled for the sun. She's wearing a bathing suit with a skirt covering her pale thighs. I know her spirit is beautiful. Rudy, she complains, could you have this picture on your wall? The naked girl, her name is Jennifer, stands by a stream. She is timid to touch the water. We see her from the side, her arms crossed over her small breasts. The light sifting through the birches glows on her skin.

It's a Watley, I answer.

Who's he?

He's a she. Sells well in New York.

To perverts. *September Morn* is art art. This is spying. Peep art, Rudy.

The painter is the girl's mother. She owns the house and spends summers in New Mexico. Jennifer lives in San Francisco. She was a couple of years ahead of me in high school. I had a crush on her. I promise to take down the picture.

When?

I'll do it now, I say. I raise the canvas from the hook and carry the picture to my car and lay it on the backseat gently. I'll hang it on my own wall until summer's over. A face to talk to.

The man with the bum ice maker, his chest strains against his shirt. He leans by the door. A tattoo covers the back of his hand. *Ve-ri-tas* written in three syllables in red on the bulging hood of a cobra. He makes a fist and the head wiggles. I went to Harvard, the man grumbles. If I'd gone to MIT, I could fix the ice maker myself.

I leave him extra trays. I explain I have to ask the owner's approval before I send someone to replace the appliance. This doesn't go over well. I spend the rest of the morning leaving messages for the owner, who lives in New Jersey. Everyone seems to live somewhere else. The afternoon I spend answering the phone and discussing rentals for October 2000. This October was booked a year ago.

So, Jimmy asks, the woman still on your mind?

I'd like to apologize to her, I answer. Tell her I'm not such a bad guy.

Sure. Then one thing will lead to another, you hope, and maybe you'll answer the underwear question.

I try to describe her to Jimmy in case he's seen her. Tall, could be a tennis player, good figure, dark hair. That's the most I can tell Jimmy without being overly specific about her legs and what else I did or didn't see.

I need more to go on, Jimmy says.

I drive home, carefully, and lean Jennifer against the wall. We danced together five years ago, a party at someone's house on the lake. The wind was chilly coming over the water and the leaves had started to turn. I told her I wasn't a very good dancer. She agreed. I told her about my crush in high school. She said she was living with a woman to find out if she liked it. She didn't know yet.

I inform Jennifer that the '38 hurricane blew the steeple off the Baptist church and flung the bandstand from the village green through the front of the hardware store across the street. Then I brush my teeth and go to bed. The woman wakes me before the birds do. I decide to spend the day driving around trying to find her.

First I visit O'Connels, the local breakfast spot. Unlikely. Usually full of Egg Beater types. I order coffee and a scone. A few tourists come in, but no one I recognize. At ten I go to Vivaldi's market. A good choice. The mist hasn't burned off yet. People are shopping early to save the rest of the day for water time when the sky clears. Lots of handsome women. Most of them with handsome men. One couple are nuzzling by the meat counter. The butcher cuts their order, a dozen New York strips. Their shopping cart is full of Sam Adams and barbecue sauce.

In the express line I keep my eye on people checking out at the other registers. The bagger drops my bananas and frozen bagels into plastic.

At the state store I replenish my Scotch supply and scan the shoppers in the wine aisles. A couple of supple ladies in their forties, tennis dresses, deep tans. I pay for Johnny Walker with a credit card, holding up the line. I apologize to a blond woman with dark eyes. She presses her Zinfandel against her chest and pretends I'm not talking to her.

I cut across the parking lot to the post office. Eleven. The mail is always up by now. People crowd into the lobby unlocking mailboxes and throwing catalogs into the recycling basket. I push my letters into my plastic, between my bagels and Johnny Walker. On my way out the door I think I see her. She's waiting in line with a priority envelope in her hand. I'm sure it's her. She's brushing her hair over her shoulder. She's contemplating the Bugs Bunny neckties next to the rack with change-of-address forms.

I read the notices on the community bulletin board and wait for her to come out so I can see her better. Consign now to the town yard sale. Buy your tickets for the Rotary lunch. Dog sitters wanted. Rides wanted. Boat for sale. Mr. Flagg from the hardware store holds the door for her. She strides toward her car. I'm sure it's the same woman. She's wearing white shorts and a loose sweater. Her sandals snap against her heels. She gets into an Isuzu Rodeo and drives away. Blue license plate. Probably Connecticut.

By the time I reach my car, hers is out of sight. I drive down the highway to Cove Road where the midrange rentals begin and start looking for her car. Mostly Subarus. A couple of Cherokees and Expeditions. The mist is thinning. The sun shines on the white gables of the Victorian at Green's Rock. She's too young for that crowd.

I drive an hour. I'm almost back to the highway. I try the dirt road to Mercy Point and there, at the last house, I see her car. I stop. The road is narrow. The ferns along the edge hide huge stones. It takes awhile to turn my car around.

Sounds like stalking to me, Jimmy says.

Jimmy, be helpful for once.

I am.

How?

What's lesson number one?

Fantasy is better than reality.

Believe it, Jimmy says.

I drive home, carefully. Pasta again. A little red wine. When I mentioned my crush, Jennifer pressed her body against mine and kissed my cheek. You should have told me before, she said. So what's your advice now? Don't listen to Jimmy, she says. I tell Jennifer I only want to tell the woman I'm sorry. Jennifer believes me.

Saturday morning I have an appointment. The couple want something for leaf season. The husband sits in the front. As we drive along I point out available houses. The child kicks the back of my seat. Sweetie, don't do that, the mother says. The woman probably has children. And a husband. Why do I care? I only want to apologize. Then I remember her Isuzu, a two-door model. Cancel children.

I make a loop and ask the couple if they'd care to see any of the houses I've pointed out. The husband thumbs the listings on his lap. What do you think, hon? The Cape with the blue shutters, hon says. I call the owner from my car phone. Sure, he says. Swing on by.

I wait in the kitchen while the owner shows the couple around. He invites me to help myself to coffee. Sweetie plays on the living room rug with a schnauzer. My wife had her ticket in her hand. She said maybe if we'd had a dog the winter days wouldn't have seemed so long. She spent a lot of them with Carl. Carl's Electric. Residential and commercial. His helpers did most of the work. Carl was a specialist. The jitney was waiting outside to take my wife to the airport. I carried her luggage to the car. We could have named the dog Carl, I said. She pretended not to hear. I'd pretended not to know.

The owner has knocked two hundred a week off the price. The schnauzer is licking sweetie's face. Light pours through the windows. Who wouldn't be happy?

In town, I buy a piece of chicken and a scoop of coleslaw at the Rotary Club tent. Profits go to the scholarship fund. The annual old-car exhibit takes up most of the green. I spend the afternoon in the office answering the phone and finishing my paperwork. At five I lock the door and wander across the street to the cars. The sky is cloudy. The owners have driven most of the cars home. The ones left all have signs saying look but don't touch. I lean over and fog the hood ornament with my breath, a winged lady, naked of course.

Jimmy pours my Scotch. I look up and see her in the mirror. She's standing in the doorway waiting for someone.

A man and another woman appear and the three of them go into the dining room. Connie, one of the servers, asks Jimmy for two Beam rocks and a vodka tonic. The lady with the black jacket and white pants, what's she drinking? The vodka tonic, Connie says. I borrow Connie's pen and a bar check. On the back I write, I apologize for almost running over you. Your drink's on me.

In a few minutes she's in the mirror again. She hands Jimmy her glass. She has thin brown fingers and polished white nails. Rings on her right hand.

I've never done that before, she says.

Jimmy mixes, pretending he's not listening.

She asks, Know what I thought?

My legs are better than hers. Watch where you're going. You might get a surprise. That's what I think you thought.

In the city you would have gotten the bird. Now I'm thinking you owe me more than a drink.

She stares at my reflection. We both look at ourselves in the mirror. I offer to buy her dinner.

Food doesn't interest me. You do, she says to my image ahead of her.

I take a deep breath. She slides off the stool and leaves her glass on the bar.

I'm with some people tonight. Come by tomorrow morning. Ten o'clock. Last house on Mercy Point. Bring a robe.

Jimmy is smiling, wiping a glass after she leaves. He says, Let's figure this out.

I'm still sober and fairly sensible. Nothing we come up with makes sense. Jennifer doesn't have a clue either. I fall asleep reading about the drought of 1900.

A clear, bright morning. A few maples are turning red. She opens the side door, barefoot and dressed in jeans and a black sweater. She tells me her name is Emily. She offers me a cup of coffee. There are some black-and-white photographs on the table by the kitchen window. Men with no clothes on.

This is what I'm here for?

The light's good this morning, Emily replies. We can work on the dock. Where's your robe?

I haven't wanted a cigarette this much in years. I tell Emily I forgot it. I remember an old raincoat in the car. That's not the way I want anyone to see me.

Emily gives me a blanket. It smells piney. I hang it over the shower rod and take off my clothes. I fold them neatly and lay them on top of the hamper.

Emily fastens her camera to a tripod. The terrace is concealed from the road and from the house next door.

The slate is warm. The sun falls over Emily's shoulder. She pushes up her sleeves and points toward the bench.

I've never done this before, I tell her.

Try to relax, Emily says.

It's not easy.

So I see.

I hope she means how I'm holding the blanket against my body. But she could mean more. I'm having a little talk with myself about that.

You've seen me, let's see you, she says. I suppose that answers the underwear question.

I stall. Tell me what I'm supposed to do.

Let's start with you lying down on the bench. Backside up.

I turn around, let the blanket go, and spread out. The slats are hot against my skin.

No good, Emily says. Stand up.

Tentatively I rise, a part of me. The other part isn't limp, but it's not erect either.

She points to a place on the dock. Kneel, she says.

It's Sunday. There won't be many boats on the water until afternoon. The boards are hard against my knees.

This is no good either, Emily says.

She tells me to lie on my back. I knew we'd come to this. I'm not happy.

Up a little bit, she says. I try not to laugh.

She suggests how to curl my body to create shadow. She rearranges her tripod and checks the light. The line of shadow goes across my thighs. The shutter clicks. She unfastens the camera and moves around my body, clicking.

Your body is better than I thought, she says. Go to a gym?

Free weights, I tell her.

A couple of more clicks. That's it, she says. All finished.

I wrap the towel around me. I ask, Are we even now?

Not until you sign a release, she answers. I show my work. I need one.

A release. There's something sexual about the word, sexual and sad and dismissive. Sometimes Jimmy is right.

She returns with the paper and a pen. I sign my name. She smiles. The first time she's done that. I'll remember it for a long time.

I'm hot in all these clothes, she says. Let's swim.

She pulls up her sweater.

I don't know why, but I say, Please don't. Light glistens on her lip.

I hope the pictures turn out. Next summer come back and tell me.

I'll send you a print.

It's not the print I care about, I tell her.

I get dressed and leave the blanket neatly folded for her to put away. It's amazing how quickly we can be somewhere else.

～ MILLY ～

On the back of the photograph of herself that Kathleen, Milly's mother, propped against Milly's pillow, she wrote, I'm going to Arizona with Ted. I know you'll be all right. I'll send you my address when I have one. Be a good girl. Have a great senior year. In her diary Milly wrote, *At least you could have told me it's not my fault. If you were a better mom, you'd know that.* Later Milly crossed out the last sentence.

Frank, Milly's father, can't figure out why she's not as angry as he is. He wants an ally, someone who will share his feelings. He can't understand what Milly feels. Frank, you lack insight, Kathleen told him often enough. Of course, she said, how could anyone who spends his time mowing fairways or hanging around the pro shop gain insight? You can learn a lot hanging around the pro shop, he'd replied. In fact Frank learned about Kathleen and Ted from a conversation he overheard in the pro shop. Doreen, the woman Frank is seeing now, says she could have told Frank herself, but it was better not to. He can't figure out why it was better not to, but he trusts Doreen.

Now, watching Milly prepare his lunch, she seems older than seventeen. Sometimes the house feels as if it was hers, as if he was a visitor and she ten years older, married, with children of her own. Dad, I'm putting sprouts on your sandwich, she says, knowing he finds them bitter. Milly! he protests. They're good for you, she says.

She runs with a crowd he doesn't approve of, kids from families with money. The boys own fast cars or vans. Doreen mentioned that the odd smell on Milly's clothes is marijuana. He's never smoked any. Doreen has. A few weeks ago he found himself imagining that Byron, Milly's boyfriend, got her pregnant. Byron's father owns the inn. He inherited money. The land the country club bought for a golf course belonged to Byron's grandfather. So it was okay then, Milly's being pregnant. Byron would marry her, give her a diamond. Byron's father would give them a nice house, perhaps not in Jeffrey, where prices are too high, but down the road in Sutton, or maybe in the other direction, Sunapee or Springfield. No, it wasn't okay. He started to cry. It was the middle of the night. He opened the door to Milly's room. She was asleep, wrapped in a white blanket. She woke up. You all right, Dad? she asked. He couldn't speak. He held her in his arms and wept. In the morning he didn't complain when Milly poured low-fat milk over his cereal.

The kitchen is small and needs painting. The whole house is small and needs painting, but Frank lives in it free, taking care of the Thorpes' house on the other side of the yard. The Thorpes spend winters in Florida. Frank keeps the road plowed and makes sure the pipes don't freeze. In summer he's sort of a handyman, when he isn't at the country club caddying or driving one of the mowers across the course. When he married Kathleen, she believed he was going to be a golf pro. He had won a couple of amateurs before dropping out of Keene State. He wanted to be a pro and play on the tour. That dream didn't pan out, like most everything else, Kathleen said. She was right, of course. Frank couldn't blame her for being disappointed. Only she had hidden her feelings so well for so long, concealed them under a layer of Irish resignation, that she took him by surprise. Sometimes he gives lessons at the club. Kathleen and Ted must have been involved with each other all the winter before the summer Ted asked for one. Frank talks to himself when he drives the big mowers, laughs out loud when he thinks about Ted asking for help for his long game. Teddy, my man, can you tee it up and knock the ball all the way from Arizona to New Hampshire? And who the hell cares anyway? At times like this, if Milly asked for advice, Frank would tell her to go ahead, marry someone who can give you diamonds. They last longer than love.

Milly is dressed in brown slacks and a white blouse. Okay to wear that? Frank asks. He's used to seeing her in her uniform.

The Thorpes are having a party, lunch and a swing band, to raise funds for home nursing. There's going to be a parade of antique cars, too. The Thorpes have hired Milly to pour wine and help the caterer pick up plates and glasses. Milly also works at the country club. She spreads clean linen on the tables, fills water glasses, sets empty dishes on trays for the busboys to carry to the kitchen. Sometimes she spends the afternoon sitting at the reception desk. A few of the older men, dozy and friendly after drinks and lunch, stop to chat and look down her dress. Be nice. They pay my salary. Yours too, Frank says.

The sky has been clouding since eleven when the drivers began to gather their antique cars on Main Street for the procession through town, then across the state road and into the Thorpes' long driveway. In the distance Mount Blue appears pale and milky in the humid air. Frank and Milly stand on their porch to watch the cars go by.

Most of the cars are black and loaded with chrome. Check that out. Frank points at a Packard, long and tall and quiet as a hearse, rolling by on enormous tires. Some cars are dark green. A couple are gray. Studebakers, Frank says, biting into his sandwich and picking sprouts from his teeth. The last car is blue, a convertible, top down, the driver's arm resting on the door, his sleeve catching the wind. The car follows the others onto the lawn in front of the Thorpes' house. The guests greet the cars with applause.

The cars circle the tent set up in the center of the lawn and park by the rhododendrons. The driver of the blue car leaves his by the rock wall, close to the wire pen where Frank used to keep a dog. It disappeared the day Kathleen left. He isn't sure if she took the dog or let it loose. Maybe it sniffed a bear and got too close and was killed, he said. Maybe it wandered through the woods and came out by the country club and one of the summer millionaires who looks down her dress took the dog home, Milly tells herself.

The band under the tent starts to play. The catering crew is passing around sandwiches and wine. Better hustle over there, Frank says.

Under the tent, men are sweating in their coats and ties. The same crowd she sees at the country club. She moves among them smiling and pouring a California red. She recognizes the man who danced with her outside the pro shop in the dark at the club's Harvest Moon Ball. He was drunk. He gave her a wet kiss and pushed some money down her blouse. A fifty-dollar bill. She keeps the money in her bureau, in the beaded party purse her mother left behind. Milly doesn't know whether the money is really hers, whether or not to spend it. The man doesn't seem to remember her, but she knows he does.

When the red is gone, Milly returns from the Thorpes' kitchen with a bottle of white. Several of the guests ask her questions to be polite: How was your summer? Do you like working at the club? Aren't you a senior this year? Are you planning on college? I'm thinking about it, she answers. She wants to go, but there isn't any money. Her father is firm about that. Annoyed, too. Milly overheard her father and Doreen talking. Her father knows its makes sense for Milly to stay in New Hampshire for her senior year, but sometimes he feels the senior year thing is an excuse. Has Kathleen ever suggested that Milly move to Arizona when she graduates? She's forgotten she has a daughter, her father grumbled. In her diary Milly wrote, *I know she'll invite me.* Later she crossed out that sentence too.

The man with the blue car, Milly sees him. Tall, slender. Thirty, maybe. Young for this crowd. Skin browner than hers. He's wearing a white linen suit and a black silk shirt, its collar open. She wishes Byron wore clothes like that. Byron prefers flannel shirts with the sleeves cut off, and shorts. He spends a fortune on hiking boots, but he never hikes anywhere, except into the woods to check the patch of ground he's cleared for his marijuana plants. He usually has a six-pack he's lifted from the cooler at the inn. She will lie beneath one of the ancient trees and let Byron feel her breasts. She pushes his hand away from her legs. When the beers are gone, Byron will stand up to urinate, complaining it's her fault he's having a difficult time. Men will tell you stuff like that, her mother explained. Tell them to relax. Byron suggests he needs some hands-on care. Milly suggests he do it himself. Sometimes he does. He looks vulnerable and ashamed afterward.

The man with the blue car chooses a sandwich from the tray and stands by himself, eating and listening to the music. He has delicate fingers. No jewelry, except for a watch with a tan leather strap. He eats quickly. She offers him wine. She feels the warmth of his skin. His eyes are deeper blue than the color of his car.

He smiles. "I never drink alone," he says.

Milly needs a second to understand what he's asking her.

"I can't," she answers.

"I understand," he says. He sounds disappointed.

Milly's body feels light, as if it's rising, or she's rising out of it. She blushes and turns away.

A few couples begin to dance, shuffling on the wooden floor set down in front of the band. She doesn't know the name of the song. She doesn't listen to music very much, but she's heard the song before, one of the tunes the people at the country club like to dance to. The wind has freshened. The canvas ripples above the dancers' heads. Clouds darken. Wind carries the smell of rain from the mountain.

Milly leaves the wine bottle next to the coffee urn and starts picking up. She carries a tray of empty glasses into the kitchen. When she returns, tapping the tray against her leg, she sees the blue car but not the driver. He's probably asked someone to dance, someone younger than forty, smartly dressed. Not many of those here. One, with dark red hair, like Milly's mother's, is talking to a man in a sport coat, Jell-O green, the color her mother said members began wearing in the sixties. Another, a blonde, a bit chunky, is standing beyond the tent smoking a cigarette. A third is dancing with an older man, who sways his shoulders against the beat of the music, keeping her off balance. No, Milly can't see the driver of the blue car anywhere.

Thunder booms from the mountain. The drivers of the old cars study the sky and confer. Doors slam. Motors start. Acrid exhaust fills the air. The cars drive way. Only an assortment of sedans and station wagons remains, and the blue convertible. When rain pelts the tent, more guests decide to leave. Suddenly the wind is blowing, the band is packing up, paper cups and napkins fly through the air, and the woman with hair the color of Milly's mother's takes off her pumps and splashes through rivulets of water to her Volvo. Rain soaks her shantung dress, which Milly covets and knows would take her years to pay for.

At last the guests are gone. The catering crew has retreated inside the house. Only Milly is outside, standing in the center of the tent, the canvas over her sagging with the weight of the downpour, looking off at the abandoned blue convertible. When the rain stops and the birds twitter among the leaves and fly down to beak worms from the sodden lawn, Milly finds some cloths, a roll of paper towels, old newspapers, and a sponge. She dries the seats first, then the dashboard and steering wheel, before she layers the newspaper on the floor. At any moment she expects the driver to reappear. Where can he be?

The caterer departs. The late-afternoon sun sparkles on the boughs of the trees and on the tresses of the chrome ornament at the tip of the hood. The key dangles from the ignition. Milly walks home and asks her father what to do. Leave the car alone, he answers. It isn't your problem.

Saturday night. Milly's father is at Doreen's house. When Milly graduates next June, she'll be expected to find a job and a place of her own. Then her father and Doreen can spend the whole night together. He won't have to come home and pretend they don't do anything but talk, eat pizza, and drink beer. *I'm glad Dad's happy. I hope Mom is too. Dad thinks I'm unhappy, but I'm not. I guess I'm just waiting, but I don't know what I'm waiting for. Maybe for someone like that guy who drove the car. I know someday I'll see him again. I know he'll remember me.*

In the moonlight the car's blue paint appears pale, almost as if what's under it is not metal at all, but cloud or water. Roomy, Byron comments about the backseat and gives her a questioning look. Always the same question, always the same answer. She shakes her head; she lets Byron kiss her. His mouth tastes like beer and cigarettes. He squeezes her breast. Don't, she says. He finishes his beer and lobs the bottle behind some birch trees. Milly opens the door and slides into the driver's seat. She finds the starter button and the knob to pull to operate the top. The motor clatters at first, then smooths out. She pulls the knob. The top rises and unfolds over her head, between her and the moonlight. She snaps the chrome handles into place, latching the top to the frame above the windshield.

Byron selects a joint from the Band-Aid can he carries them in. Milly won't let him sit in the car. He leans against the door. He offers her some smoke. She shakes her head. How come? Byron asks. But she doesn't answer. Doesn't tell him she's traveling down a road somewhere with the man who drove the car to the party. His hand rests softly on her thigh. She spreads her fingers where he has his. Byron is watching her. Let me help, he says. She rolls up the window and pushes the door open, Byron's cue to leave.

A week goes by. The pines drop needles over the car. Milly brushes them off. She lifts the hem of the uniform she's worn home from working Saturday lunch at the club and polishes the chrome rings around the headlights. Another week. The mowers come. Their machines blow dust and clippings onto the fenders. Milly fills a bucket with water and rinses the car clean. Soon school begins. In the evening, before her father gets home, Milly starts the engine and sits in the car watching the temperature needle inch toward the center of the gauge. Why doesn't Mr. Thorpe do something about the car? she wonders. Perhaps he and the driver are friends and it's okay to leave the car there.

The maples turn red. The town is full of leaf peepers. The guidance counselor inquires about Milly's plans. Car sitting, she replies. What about college? he asks. No money, she says. She remembers the hand in her blouse. Well, fifty dollars, she says. Phone your mother, her father says. Milly dials information and tells the operator Phoenix, but she isn't sure what name her mother is using. Try Ong, Milly says. There aren't any, the voice tells her. Then check Boyer, Milly says. Too many Boyers to decide. Milly hangs up. She writes a letter, mails it to the address on the one her mother sent her.

The end of October is full of storms. Milly cleans the fallen leaves off the car. The sun comes out. Milly sits in the car. The air smells like dust and someone's sweat. She imagines pressing her cheek against the man's brown skin. His fingers stroke her hair. *Where has he gone? Why hasn't he come back? What could have happened?*

November. Dear Milly, I want to help but I can't. Ted doesn't want me to work and I don't want to ask him for money. His business is slow to catch on here. You know, the new guy on the block stuff. How are you? Milly writes back, I'm fine, but the car won't start anymore.

In December Milly abandons the car to the snow.

That winter Mr. Thorpe dies in Florida. Mrs. Thorpe returns to Jeffrey in June with Mr. Thorpe in a small cardboard box. Milly is graduated from high school. Under her yearbook photograph no awards or activities are listed, no college choices. But someone has written, Bound to go far.

Mrs. Thorpe buys a condo, scatters her husband's ashes over the golf course, and informs Milly's father he has to find another place to live.

He and Doreen move to Sunapee, five miles away. Byron's father offers Milly a waitressing job at the inn. Milly rents an apartment above the Stop 'n Go on Main Street with Michelle, who graduated a year earlier and works checkout at Vivaldi's market.

One summer night, after the dining room closes, Milly wonders if anyone has moved the blue car. Byron has a new van. Milly sits in the backseat. Michelle and Byron smoke some of the leaf from last year's crop, an open box of Mallomars on the console between them.

The moon is out, the car lies in deep shadow. The windows are smashed. One of the doors hangs open. She knows most of the names sprayed on the fenders. The top is shredded. The fog lights are cracked, the seats slit. They give off the odor of mold.

Milly feels the car grieving, feels its shame, its humiliation. She touches the tip of the hood. Someone had pried away the ornament.

Byron pisses on the grass, shakes himself off, and drives everyone back to town.

II

Since dropping out of Juilliard, Paul has made his way playing piano at events and parties, the Hamptons in summer, Manhattan in winter. He played for the

Walters many times. Bernie, Dr. Walter, was several years older than his wife, Veronica, called Ronnie by her husband, her friends, and one or two headwaiters. Late in the evening, after the guests departed and Bernie had removed his hearing aid and gone to bed, she often asked Paul to stay a little longer. She would sit beside him as he played, by that time in the early morning, improvising and nursing the Scotch Ronnie had mixed for him. Her head would rest on his shoulder. Paul was twenty years younger, at least, than Ronnie, but he didn't have sex very often, and he suspected she never did with Bernie anymore. So Paul didn't object when Ronnie started sharing his Scotch. They made love twice before Bernie died. Both of Paul's parents had died. She was grateful to Paul for helping her to arrange Bernie's funeral.

A month later Ronnie asked Paul to drive her car to Florida. She would fly down and he could help her open the house in Naples that Bernie used to describe as a fixer-upper he bought for a hundred thousand, now worth two million and counting. Ronnie pressed a wad of bills into Paul's hand. So now you're a kept man, he told himself, wondering whether he had come up in the world or gone down. He would go along with Ronnie's proposition and see what happened. That was the way he lived his life. He guessed she would find someone her own age, someone with money and the right credentials for going out with in public. Ronnie had endured the gossip of Bernie's friends, who suspected her of marrying him for his money. She wasn't going to provoke more comment by being seen with a piano player as much younger than herself as she had been younger than Bernie.

Paul arrived in Naples in November. He shopped, made salads for lunch, mixed cocktails, called the plumber and the air-conditioning man, waxed the car, and played the piano after dinner. Ronnie sat on the lanai and listened. Later she would kiss Paul's fingers and press them to her breast and they would make love in her room, in the round bed, on beige sheets. The next morning, Ronnie would ask Paul to put fresh sheets on the bed and wash the others. Paul played things her way, whether it was "Liebesträume" night after night or removing the evidence so she didn't feel Bernie's disapproving gaze from above.

When the season got under way, Ronnie often spent evenings at the Pelican Club, where Bernie had been a member. Paul, darling, she said, I shouldn't be selfish. He knew she meant don't count on things staying the way they are. Lots of other widows could use someone like you, she said.

When Ronnie's New York friends visited, Paul disappeared to a motel near the airport. Planes roared overhead, shadowing the pool and the narrow horseshoe of cement where Paul sunned and considered his future. He had a business card printed: confidentially yours, his name lower left in raised ink. Soon his calendar was full. He drove women to their doctor's appointments, to their hairdressers, to their clubs; gave advice about which wines to buy, which garages could be trusted (he was guessing, of course); bought presents for grandchildren and stood in lines at the post office. He checked out books from the library and returned them; he drove to funerals; he kissed cheeks; he gave instructions on setting burglar alarms and unsetting them; and more than once, when asked, he stayed overnight. He was also playing the piano again at parties.

Ronnie now went out with several men. She introduced Paul to one of them who needed a favor. Paul drove to Miami and picked up a package. A piece of pre-Columbian pottery, the man explained when he unwrapped it. The artifact's journey hadn't been entirely a legal one, Paul suspected. The buyer tipped Paul five hundred dollars. Another man asked Paul to deliver some documents to Houston and gave Paul another five hundred. Then Paul met Everett McCord. The McCords lived in a pink, Spanish-style house on one of the canals close to the bay. Any of the ten bathrooms in the pink house was larger than Paul's motel room.

My wife admires your playing, McCord said.

It's passable, Paul answered.

She thinks it's better than that, McCord said. She has difficulty sleeping. She thinks you might help her.

A little night music? Paul asked.

McCord didn't smile. Something like that. Recordings don't seem to work.

What's your wife's name?

Elise, McCord said.

For Elise, then. Paul smiled at his joke even if McCord didn't.

Several evenings a month Paul sat in the music room on the second floor of the pink house. The music drifted down the hallway of Persian rugs and Cuban tile into the room whose door was always open and where, Paul assumed, listened Elise McCord. He had never actually seen her at home, only her portrait downstairs in the library. Paul remembered the woman whose face matched the one looking down from the wall, her throat encircled by a handsome necklace. Paul had seen her at several parties. She preferred not the gown with its low neck that she wore in the portrait, but dark suits and dresses that concealed her tall figure. She pinned up her hair. Paul remembered how her eyes concentrated on his hands.

The way the piano was arranged in the music room, Paul sat with his back to the hallway and the open door. An enormous mirror in several panels spread across the wall. One night Paul glanced up from his playing and encountered the reflection of Elise McCord standing in the doorway of her room. She appeared only an instant, yet long enough for Paul to take in the shadow of her body under the nightgown she wore, which was as white as the keys under his hands. Paul was so struck by what he had seen that he lost his place in the music and riffed the melody before he found his way again.

Later that evening, a check for a month's work in his pocket, Paul stood on the lawn and stared at the lighted window in the room he thought was the one Elise McCord listened in. A patrol car stopped. The officer shined a light on Paul and asked what he was doing there. The officer examined the check McCord had written and Paul's driver's license. Satisfied, the officer still escorted Paul off the lawn and watched Paul get into his well-worn Honda Civic. You don't make much, do you? the officer commented.

Humiliated, Paul drove home. The officer had seen into the very heart of Paul's existence. He was an errand boy, no different from the kid who delivered pizzas and sold Paul the car. One chance was what Paul wanted, one opportunity to make some real money. He would be different then. He was sure of it. But it was May, and the Naples crowd was packing up to go north. Paul had few prospects for the summer.

Paul inquired if the McCords needed someone to watch over the pink house during the summer. I have another idea, McCord said.

He owned a house in New Hampshire. Mrs. McCord loved it there in August. They were going to Europe for two months first. Paul could go up in July and get things ready. Jeffrey was the name of the town. The house was on a lake. McCord gave Paul the house keys and a list of things to do.

III

By six every morning, sunlight filled Paul's room. Birds sang in the spruce boughs. From his window he could see the lake sparkle beyond the birches. Paul felt at ease, at peace. He had the piano tuned and wrote a couple of songs.

One by one Paul accomplished the tasks on McCord's list. He unstored the Mercedes coupé, which McCord had given him permission to use. There was also a Scout. He had a service clean the house. The paving company resurfaced the driveway. He activated the charge account at the market. The pool service rolled off the winter cover, scrubbed the tiles, changed the water, and balanced the chemicals. The marina towed McCord's boat to his boathouse. Paul ordered a case of McCord's favorite California white from the state store, and arranged with the mechanic who maintained McCord's collection of antique cars in the barn up the slope of the yard from the boathouse to have the cars ready for McCord's arrival. A lady phoned to remind Mr. McCord that he had promised to drive one of his cars to a fund-raiser for the Home Nursing Association.

The McCords arrived by limousine from Logan airport. Elise wore linen trousers and a suede jacket. She took off her sunglasses and said hello to Paul, the first time she had actually spoken to him. Her eyes were red. She turned away and walked toward the house. McCord had on a tan summer suit and a blue shirt. He looked jowlier than Paul remembered.

McCord followed his wife into the house, leaving the luggage for Paul, except for one piece Elise seemed to guard. Paul had been sleeping in the servant's room over the kitchen and didn't know whether McCord expected him to stay or move out, or if McCord had any more jobs in mind for Paul to do, other than carrying the luggage inside.

After a look around, McCord said, I knew I could count on you. Then he explained that the cook needed Paul's room. She'll be here tomorrow. I think you'll be comfortable at the inn. Please use the Scout, McCord said.

While he talked he kept looking over his shoulder, as if he expected Elise to be watching. Let's have a chat tomorrow, McCord said.

Sedans with New York and Florida license plates filled the inn's parking lot. The elderly faces in the dining room seemed so familiar that Paul thought he knew everyone. He nodded politely, and guests nodded back. But he knew no one there. Despite their ages and some obvious infirmities, he envied them, their comfort, their ease at the end of their lives. How dreary he imagined his own would be.

The next day McCord found Paul. They walked across the green. Workers were erecting tents for the annual flower show. Shirtless men drove stakes into the ground to secure the ropes. The ring of sledges sounded eerie and hollow.

Let me talk openly, McCord said. Elise's lover is younger than I am. I made my money. He inherited his. She thinks I don't know about them. He's given her a diamond necklace, larger than the one in her portrait. A case of mine's bigger than yours. Know what I mean?

McCord's sudden chumminess surprised Paul, and irritated him.

A down payment on the future, I suppose, McCord continued. There's a false bottom in her jewelry box. You'll see a little catch to open it. I want you to take the necklace and give it to me.

Take? You mean steal?

Borrow. Eventually she'll get it back. I want to see her stew for a while. I'll pay you a thousand.

How much is the necklace worth?

Fifty thousand, at least.

A ten percent tip, at least?

Five thousand then.

Paul felt pleased with himself. How do I do it? he asked.

I added a car to my collection last year. A Caddie convertible. Blue's not the right color, but it looks nice.

I saw it, Paul said.

No one else has. I like to surprise people. You drive it to a party. Elise doesn't like old cars, but I promised I'd bring one. She and I will come over in the Mercedes. You take the necklace, drive the old car to the party, hide the necklace in the car, and walk away. I'll drive the car home.

It's taking the necklace I'm worried about, Paul said.

Be at the house at eleven. We'll be out doing errands. The cook won't be there either. You have a house key. Elise keeps the jewelry box in her lingerie drawer. Drive the old car to the inn and go from there.

I don't know . . .

Paul, I'm not planning the perfect crime here. In fact, it's not a crime at all. Elise will get her necklace back. She'll just have to make a few admissions. Anyway, what can she do when she finds it's missing? She's not going to phone the police or the insurance company. The necklace is a secret, remember?

Saturday morning Paul woke to the patter of rain, but later the sun worked through the clouds. Humid air stuck to his skin. The Mercedes was gone. Paul unlocked the door. He stood for a minute smelling the damp odor of old wood mixed with the metallic smell that blew off the lake. He remembered a chapel by a lake when he was young, near Seneca, where his parents spent summer vacations. He remembered a priest named Bullit, who let Paul practice on the church's piano. God loves a musical soul, Bullit said. At this moment Paul felt no music in himself at all.

He climbed the stairs. He knew the rooms. He had opened the closets and drawers before, clothes neatly folded or hung waiting for the McCords to return. Paul knew which bureau to look in. The drawer slid open.

He smelled cedar sachet now. He lifted the box tenderly and almost with anguish peered down at the delicate shapes and soft colors that Elise put next to her body. He set the box beside twin silver hairbrushes engraved with Elise's initials. He pressed the catch on the side of the box. It opened. The weight of the necklace flowed over Paul's fingers.

Maybe he caught the fragrance of her soap and then raised his face to the mirror above the bureau, or maybe it was only after he saw her that he smelled the buttery scent from her skin. Elise was standing behind him holding a towel against her chest. His breathing stopped, the way it stopped when he had seen her in the doorway.

Please don't, she said. Please . . .

Paul trembled. He made a fist, the necklace in it. Then he ran.

The car started. The breeze across his damp shirt chilled Paul's skin. He pulled into the line of old cars on Main Street. While he waited for the procession to start, he hunched down. Scraping his knuckles on the metal under the dashboard, he loosened the top of the panel behind the emergency brake and pulled the panel loose, wide enough for his hand to get by. He let go of the necklace, heard it drop, and pushed the panel back into place.

What was the party for? Some sort of charity thing, but he couldn't remember which one. He parked near some rhododendrons. Someone asked him what year his car was. Nineteen forty, he answered. McCord had told him that. The man leaned closer and peered inside. Paul walked toward the tent in the center of the lawn. A band started to play. The song was familiar, but he couldn't remember its name. Paul drank a glass of wine. He began to feel calm again. He looked into the face of a young woman. She had bright eyes and freckles across her nose. She seemed nice and stayed beside him while he sipped a second glassful. He wanted her to drink wine too, but she couldn't. She was working there. She kept looking at him.

Over the mountain the sky darkened. Paul heard thunder. Fifteen or twenty minutes, McCord said it would take Paul to walk to the inn. He wanted to say good-bye to the young woman. She was busy picking up now. He crossed the highway. He could smell the rain behind him.

By Wednesday McCord hadn't called to set up a time to meet. Paul wanted the money McCord had promised. Paul considered phoning McCord but decided against it. Paul spent his days walking from one end of town to the other, returning to the inn to check for messages. He took long naps. If he couldn't sleep, he thought about the young woman who had stood next to him. A beautiful face, innocent, full of expectation. He thought about Elise, that he had betrayed her, the woman who had taken his breath away, whom he had waited in the dark to see pass in front of her window, a woman who was beyond him, whom he could never approach as an equal. Had he betrayed her for their differences or for the money? When Paul passed the piano in the lobby, he felt ashamed.

On Friday Paul bought the new edition of the town's weekly newspaper. He sat at the bar drinking a Manhattan, skimming the articles. The words were on the second page, near the bottom, words that focused all his attention. Woman's death called accidental. Everett McCord, a summer resident, returned to his house on the lake late Saturday morning and discovered his wife at the bottom of the stairs. She had apparently fallen. EMTs Allen Noise and Laura Trimpi attempted to revive her but were unsuccessful. On Tuesday the medical examiner ruled Mrs. McCord died of a heart attack. McCord confirmed that his wife suffered from a heart condition. The medical examiner cannot say whether the condition led to a fall or a fall caused her heart to fail. McCord made a search of the house with Deputy Rolli London. McCord noted his wife's jewelry box was open on her bureau in the bedroom. Nothing was missing, McCord told London. A service for Mrs. McCord will be held later this year in Naples, Florida, the article concluded.

Paul looked around the room to see if anyone was watching him. He realized he had been staring at the article for several minutes. Paul folded the paper. She must have fallen down the stairs chasing him. Whether heart failed first or not didn't matter.

While Paul drank his second Manhattan, some other thoughts began to nag him. McCord said Elise would be out. Did he plan for her not to be? McCord knew what might happen if she discovered Paul stealing the necklace. If she had not suffered a heart attack, would Paul have been set up to be caught and charged with burglary? How could he convince anyone that McCord had put him up to it? Certainly I haven't paid him anything, McCord would say, I asked him to drive my car to the lunch, that's all. A search of the car would turn up the necklace.

Paul drank his third Manhattan and tried to decide what to do. The only thing he could figure out was to go back to Florida and wait for the season to change and for Mrs. Walter and her friends to go south again, and for him to pick up where he had left off before he ever met McCord.

By September Paul was almost out of money. The resort season was still weeks away. He put an ad in the newspaper and was hired to give some piano lessons. He took a job delivering the paper, too.

He delivered to the Port Royal section. The pink house was on his route. In October the discreet real estate sign appeared at the edge of the lawn. Paul phoned the agent, pretending to be interested, saying he was a friend of McCord. The owner had suffered a tragedy and was going to live abroad, the agent informed Paul. I know Mrs. McCord died, Paul said.

Yes, there you have it, the agent said. As far as Paul could determine, no memorial service for Elise McCord was ever held, not in Naples, anyway.

When Mrs. Walter returned, she was no longer Mrs. Walter. She had married a retired optometrist. They didn't require Paul's services. Only a few of the others Paul had helped gave him work again. He depended on his paper route to get by. He started out in the dark. Soon the first streaks of dawn appeared. The streets were quiet and empty. Mist shrouded the trees. Sprinklers clicked back and forth. Grass sparkled in the beams of his lights. Sometimes he stopped in front of the pink house. He sat in the car while he rolled papers and slid them into plastic bags, which he pulled one by one from the sleeve of them hanging from the car's rearview mirror. The people who delivered papers came and went all the time. Always a new face waiting in the parking lot for the bundles. We're all drifters, Paul thought. Florida is full of drifters, people from somewhere else with no other place to go. Jeffrey wasn't like that. He ought to go back to Jeffrey.

But the rhythm of his life is persuasive, hard to change. In summer Naples has hundreds of empty houses. Paul becomes a professional caretaker. Year after year the same pattern: a house in the summer, then the weather turning cool again, the snowbirds returning, the extra jobs to do. If he's lucky, he finds a boat to live on during the winter. A life with conveniences and no future. He's used to it. However, on his fortieth birthday, on his fourth Manhattan, he finally decides it's time to leave.

IV

Milly stands in the Jeffrey post office holding the letter. Through the window, she can see Susie, her daughter, sitting in her car seat laughing because Spook, part Lab and part something else, is licking her face.

The letter is from District Court. Jury duty. Just what I need, she says. It means hours away from the gym and driving to Concord in a car with a leaky radiator and tires that won't pass the next inspection. Her regulars have all returned now, from Florida and Arizona, tanned and pounds heavier than when they left in the fall. Her morning aerobics class is full. But it's the clients who pay for personal training that she counts on, the ones she encourages on the weight machines and guides through stretching routines. They're the ones who pay the bills, clients in their sixties and seventies, years without doing exercise. Milly charges fifty dollars an hour. Some of the men don't really want to work out. They're following doctor's orders, grumbling about the effort. What does it matter? they ask. Too late, they say, to change anything. But they like looking at Milly in her spandex, like talking to her, telling her what they used to do when they weren't old. They have no one else to tell their stories to. They remind her of the men at the country club who flirted and looked down her dress. They still do that, her clients, but she understands now. They're strangers in their own bodies.

On the morning Milly must present herself for the jury pool, she leaves Susie at preschool and drives the thirty miles south to Concord. The hills shine with summer green. Hard to imagine how deep the snow lay during the winter.

The court is in a new building a few minutes off the interstate. A man in a brown uniform holds out a tray for keys. Just like going on a plane, someone says. Milly has never been on a plane, has never needed to fly anywhere, though once she drove to Logan Airport to see off her mother, who was flying from Boston to London with Ted for a second honeymoon.

Milly passes through the metal detector. If you're selected to serve, tell the judge you're a single parent. He'll excuse you, one of Milly clients had advised her. She knew what he meant, but it sounded as if the man, who is given to staring at Milly's breasts, was suggesting that the judge would excuse her for becoming pregnant. If anyone wants to know, Milly will tell them it wasn't an accident.

The air-conditioning chills the hallway where Milly sits with the others called for duty. She's glad she brought a sweater. No one talks. Finally a bailiff leads the group into a courtroom. The judge enters. The group rises and sits down again. In the front of the room are two tables. One of the attorneys has a braid of black hair. Next to him sits a man wearing a white shirt and brown jacket. She has seen him before.

Milly scans the people at the other table: a man in a dark shirt with a bright tie, and an elderly woman. The post office in Jeffrey. Milly has seen her there. She talks to herself while she opens her mail. Sometimes she takes out a magnifier and bends over her mail to make out what it says.

The man at the first table. Milly studies him. Yes, of course. The man who drove the blue car. Milly's sure it's the same person. Older now, thinner maybe, but not that different.

Ladies and gentleman, the judge begins. He explains the case. It involves a charge of criminal trespass and the unlawful taking of a canoe.

The charge is brought by Mrs. Helen Hanford, a resident of Jeffrey, New Hampshire, the judge continues. The defendant is Mr. Paul Kennedy, recently living in Florida and now residing in Jeffrey, New Hampshire.

A door opens. A woman walks toward a box and begins drawing names.

Adele Kruger, the woman announces.

The person seated in front of Milly stands up.

The judge asks Ms. Kruger if she knows any of the parties or anyone representing them or has heard comments about the case. She hasn't, she answers.

Can you serve? the judge asks.

I can, she says.

The bailiff motions for her to follow him. He points to the first empty chair in the jury section opposite the attorneys.

Other names are called; other jurors are seated.

Millicent Ong, the woman calls out.

Milly stands up. I'm a single mother, she could tell the judge. Or, she could say, I poured the accused, at least I think it's him, a glass of wine at a party once. He wore beautiful clothes and drove a blue convertible. It was beautiful too. I wanted to talk to him. He wanted to talk to me. But I couldn't. We couldn't. I've thought of him a lot.

Ms. Ong, can you serve?

I can, Milly answers.

She takes the last chair, no more than a few feet away from the accused. She wants to turn to look at him to find out if he's looking at her. She doesn't dare. She keeps her attention on the judge, who is conferring with the attorneys. Each side accepts the jurors selected. The judge sets the trial day for the following Monday.

Marcie, who is divorced and doesn't have children, comes to supper at Milly's. The house Milly rents on Dutchman's Hill used to be a studio. The sweet pungent smell of mock orange comes through the open window.

Marcie manages the Cove, a restaurant popular with the summer people. She brings two bottles of wine.

When they finish the first one, Milly puts Susie to bed. Later, after Marcie leaves, Milly will unfold the couch and move Susie there. Spook will settle beside Milly into the warm place where Susie had been sleeping.

Most of the people I cared about drifted out of my life, Milly says. This guy drifts into it again.

Milly's mother sends her a small check every birthday. Milly's father and Doreen have moved to Vermont. He phones at Christmas. Every now and then Doreen sends Susie something to wear.

What was to care about? You turned around and he was gone, Marcie says. Now you find out he's a guy who steals canoes.

We don't know that.

You don't know much else about him, either.

He made me feel funny when I saw him.

Funny how? Like weak in the knees? Like he was going to sweep you off your feet and take you away in that old car that got trashed?

No, Milly thinks, back then she never wanted to go away. That's what other people did. I expected something from him, she says. But I can't tell you what it was. I just did.

Did you think he was rich?

I guess I was wrong. Anyway, I still think about him.

I never met anyone like that.

I haven't met anyone else like that.

Milly fills Marcie's wineglass. They finish the pizza.

How many times do you think he's thought about you?

Probably none.

Probably.

On Monday the jurors gather at nine o'clock. The bailiff informs them that the attorneys and the judge are conferring. The jurors pick through a stack of tattered magazines and drink coffee. An hour passes before the bailiff escorts the jurors into the courtroom. Milly doesn't see either Mrs. Hanford or Mr. Kennedy, only their attorneys.

Ladies and gentlemen, the judge says, your service will not be needed this morning. The charges have been withdrawn. The State of New Hampshire excuses you and thanks you for your willingness to serve.

Milly returns to Jeffrey and phones the clients she canceled to rebook them.

I know Helen Hanford, Marge London says.

Marge London, whose son Rolli used to be one of the town's deputies, is bent over a plump green ball doing leg lifts.

Helen's confused. She doesn't remember where her property line is, Marge says, sliding off the ball and turning onto her back.

Marge talks and does sit-ups. Her voice sounds throaty and breathless.

The man lives in a trailer home on the McDevitt property next door. Helen leaves out the canoe for her grandson to use.

Marge's face and shoulders are turning red. One more, Milly says.

When he got through he beached it over the line, Marge manages to say out of the corner of her mouth.

She lies on the exercise mat patting her stomach. Mind you, the man did use the canoe without asking. His name rang a bell with my son. Paul Kennedy. He worked for that Mr. McCord, the one whose wife fell down the stairs and died. Remember?

Don't think so.

McCord had a house on the lake. He was shopping one Saturday and came home and found his wife at the bottom of the stairs. Not a stitch on.

She fell?

Had a heart attack and fell, or fell and had the attack. A doctor in Florida confirmed she suffered heart problems. My son thought she'd chased somebody out of the house. There was a damp bath towel in the hall upstairs like she'd dropped it running. Someone peeping at her maybe, or someone got in to steal something. Stealing was what my son thought. There was an open jewelry box in a bedroom. If she'd discovered a peeper, she'd probably lock herself in and phone for help with her condition, not chase the person with nothing on but a towel and lose that. McCord said this Paul Kennedy had worked for him but wasn't staying there. They also employed a cook. She had the day off. McCord said nothing was taken, so my son never spoke with the man. The whole thing didn't sit right with my son, though.

Milly helps Marge to her feet and leads her to a tall machine called the assisted pull-up. Milly sets the weight. Marge stands on the movable step, her hands gripping the bar above her head.

Do five if you can, Milly says.

Milly usually counts while Marge goes up and down. This time she doesn't. She's thinking about what Marge said.

Four's it for me today, Marge says. She wipes her face with the towel Milly hands her.

Does Mr. McCord still live here?

No. He sold his cars and his house and left as soon as he could after his wife died.

Cars?

He collected some old ones. Drove them around town. I bet you saw one.

I bet I did, Milly tells herself.

Paul is having a drink at the bar at the inn. He likes to have a drink there in the evening when the regulars assemble after closing their shops and offices. He can tell who's a regular by the way they talk to Jimmy. Paul likes to think he's one too. By now Jimmy doesn't have to ask, but mixes Paul a Manhattan as soon as he sits down.

Paul would like to buy everyone a drink and be his friend. He delivers the *Concord Monitor* in the morning and teaches a couple of beginning students an hour a week. He can't afford to buy anyone a drink. So he drinks by himself and thinks about the juror, the one who had that odd last name. She has to be the woman who poured his wine at the party he drove the car to. Has to be.

An August morning. Paul stops his car to watch a pair of loons. Mist hangs over the lake. The trees along the roadside cast thin gray shadows. A runner is coming toward him over a hill. A baroque piece is playing on the radio. Handel, Paul thinks. The rhythm of the runner, the motion of arms and legs, goes with the music, as if the melody was written for the runner's accompaniment. Closer, Paul recognizes the face under the hat. The runner glances at the windshield, runs past, stops. Paul opens the door. He stands in the shadows of the trees. Milly walks back to him.

It is you, isn't it? Milly asks.

In court, you mean?

No. The party. You drove the blue car. We spoke. I was pouring wine. From his smile, Milly knows she's right.

Paul explains he delivers papers and stopped to watch some loons. He asks if Milly lives on the lake.

Not on what I earn, she answers, and tells Paul she works at the fitness center.

I need to finish my route, Paul says. Maybe we could get together.

Ong. There's only one in the phone book, Milly answers.

A week later Paul calls to invite Milly to Sunday brunch at the inn. Marcie baby-sits Susie.

Why didn't you come back for the car? Milly asks.

Paul explains that the man he worked for was supposed to be at the party and drive the car home.

You mean Mr. McCord? Milly asks.

You knew him?

I've heard of him.

I opened his house while he and his wife were in Europe. He didn't need me anymore after they arrived. I drove the car as a favor before I went back to Florida.

You know what happened to his wife?

I read it in the paper.

I suppose that's why he didn't show up.

Milly and Paul finish their meal.

Paul asks about Susie. Milly tells him that Susie's father lives in Vermont with the woman he said he was going to leave.

The second time Paul invites Milly to dinner, they eat at the Cove, at one of the tables outside. By the time they finish their wine, the sky is full of stars. Milly tells Paul how she tried to take care of the car but some kids tore it up.

Paul asks what finally happened to the car.

I think it got towed to Sunapee, Milly says.

She tells him there's a junkyard. She can't remember the name of the street, but you come down the long hill into town and turn right at the firehouse, she says.

What was she like, Mrs. McCord? Milly asks when Paul invites her to dinner again. This time at his trailer. He cooks burgers on a grill. Paul and Milly take their plates and sit on the dock. The sun is going down. It's almost September.

Elise, Paul says. Her name was Elise. I played piano at some parties in Florida. She had trouble sleeping. Her husband hired me to come to their house and play a few evenings a month. He thought it would help her.

Did it?

I don't know. But I don't think so.

Were the McCords happy?

I thought they were, but they weren't.

Milly thinks she shouldn't bring up what Marge said, but decides to anyway. Marge London is a client of mine. Her son used to be one of the town's deputies. She said he was never sure what really happened.

I only know what I read in the paper.

Milly picks up the plates and takes them into the trailer to wash. She notices Paul's keyboard.

I quit playing. I'm getting into it again, he says.

He kisses her. She kisses him back.

McCord told me Elise had a lover.

Milly traces Paul's mouth with her fingers. It wasn't you, was it?

She liked my piano. That's all.

Would you play something for me?

I'm out of practice, Paul says.

Sunapee is only a few miles away. Paul drives down the hill into town. There's the firehouse Milly mentioned, the turn onto the street Milly couldn't remember the name of. It's called Sugar Road. It winds along the river. Paul passes a church, some houses with blankets hung over porch railings, an old garage, then a machine shop before he sees a field with stunted apple trees and several wooden boats leaning on their sides and a few rusted cars almost hidden by weeds.

A wire fence surrounds the field. The gate is open. There's a one-room concrete building, a note on the door: BACK IN THIRTY MINUTES.

Paul walks around the building and into the field. September now. The sun warms his face. Grasshoppers with folded wings sway on the weeds. Crickets cheep in the tangled grass. The air is dusty with drying leaves. Paul smells the tang of roots and fallen apples.

He sees the car. It's mostly blue. The hood leans against the door on the driver's side. The motor is gone, the chrome strips and bumpers too. The tire treads have split apart.

Paul pulls on the passenger-side door. The hinges snap. The seats are slit and moldy. Birds have built nests above the visors. Snakes have eaten the birds. One snake has shed its skin across the hump in the floor. Paul kneels down and inches under the dash until he can reach the panel where he hid the necklace. He grips the top. The panel pulls away. The necklace is there, coiled where he dropped it. Paul pockets the necklace and returns to his car as fast as he can.

Down the street he has to pull over. His arms and legs are quivering. He gets out of the car and walks around, takes deep breaths. He manages to drive to the inn. The lunch crowd is gathering, mostly iced-tea drinkers. Jimmy fixes a Manhattan. Paul needs two before he stops shaking. It takes an hour to make up his mind.

What's it worth, do you think? Milly asks.

Way into five figures. What would you buy with that much money?

Milly remembers the fifty dollars the man pushed down her dress. She'd kept the money a year, then bought a winter coat with it.

For starters, I'd pay off the loans I took out to send myself to school. Then I'd save for Susie's college, so she can go if she has the chance.

This is different though. The fifty dollars was hers. The necklace isn't. And it isn't Paul's either. In fact, he seems afraid of it. Maybe we both are, Milly thinks. Both stare at the necklace lying in the center of the small table Paul bought at the Goodwill store in Concord.

You want to try it on? Paul asks.

Milly shakes her head.

They hear the car outside. Paul opens the trailer door and watches the man cross the grass. Rollie London. He's short, with broad shoulders and gray hair. He owns a security company now. Paul asked Milly to phone him.

Rollie shakes Paul's hand.

Come in, Paul says.

Rollie greets Milly and looks at the necklace.

Sorry there's not more room to sit down, Paul apologizes.

I don't mind standing, Rollie says.

I worked for the McCords once. I think you remember.

I remember, Rollie says. I had my eye on you.

I worked for them in Florida first. They went to Europe and I came up here and got their house ready for them. Mr. McCord told me his wife's lover gave her this necklace.

Paul explains what McCord asked him to do.

If she followed me, I didn't hear her, Paul says.

But she might have, Rollie says.

She might have, Paul agrees.

McCord returned a few minutes after you left. Maybe she confronted him and he pushed her.

Why didn't McCord ever come for his car? Milly asks.

Rollie starts to give a policeman's explanation. Paul interrupts. McCord didn't care, Paul says. The car and the necklace didn't matter to him. He had what he wanted.

V

They were never as close again, Milly and Paul, as that afternoon. Paul had asked who the necklace belonged to. Certainly not to McCord. It didn't exist in his version of things. The town's attorney would be the one to decide, but Rollie supposed the man who owned the property in Sunapee where Paul found the car had a claim. If Mrs. McCord had any relatives, they'd probably have one too.

The town's attorney will want to know how I got the necklace, Paul said.

I imagine he will, Rollie responded.

I'd prefer not to tell him.

You take the necklace to his office or you don't, Rollie said. I'm not going to ask.

Rollie drove away. Paul walked across the yard, beyond a row of spruces. He had the necklace in his pocket.

A few minutes later Milly saw Paul in a canoe on the water. I asked this time, he said.

There was another paddle. Paul steadied the canoe and Milly seated herself in the bow. He steered the canoe toward the center of the lake.

Paul rested his paddle across his knees. The canoe bobbed up and down. Paul took the necklace from his pocket. He stretched out his hand, the necklace in his palm.

Last chance, he said. Yours if you want it.

I don't, she said.

Okay then, Paul said.

He swung his arm over his head. The necklace sparkled in the air. Then it lay upon the water. Then it disappeared.

Milly stopped looking and took up her paddle. Paul guided the canoe toward the shore.

The sky had lost its brilliance. Clouds hid the summit of Mount Blue. Winter wasn't far away. The mood of the season mixed with the sadness of realizing Paul wasn't a mystery anymore. The man in a silk shirt driving a blue convertible that he abandoned in the rain was a nice guy who delivered newspapers. He wanted to settle down. Live the rest of his life in Jeffrey.

Milly remembered her mother at the airport. She looked great. Ted was really my prince, she said, snuggling against him. He rescued me.

Milly guessed she would live the rest of her life in Jeffrey too, but maybe not with anyone. Not with Paul, anyway.

When Susie is older, Milly will tell her a man threw some diamonds into the lake. She will even point out where it happened. Susie will say, Mom, you're making it up.

You're right. I'm making it up, Milly will answer. But think about diving down one day and coming back with a handful of diamonds. Suddenly your whole life will change.

Tears will fill Susie's eyes. I don't want my life to change, she will say.

I never wanted mine to change either, Milly will say.

～ PRIVACY ～

"Is that George?" Hank asked.

Hank pointed to a person seated at the end of a pew near the front of the church, the place where George usually sat. The gray hair looked like George's. This morning instead of George's familiar yellow sweater, Kate observed the rounded collar of a blue dress. Madge, George's wife, used to wear a dress like that to cocktail parties. Kate remembered the white buttons. Madge had a pair of dark blue-and-white pumps that went well with the dress.

"I think it is," Kate whispered.

The person in the blue dress turned to let someone go by. No doubt about it: George.

"What the hell is he doing?" Hank whispered.

Kate was wondering what shoes he was wearing. Madge was a large woman. She referred to herself as full figured. George was slim. Kate didn't think Madge's pumps would fit him.

The church was the small, stone Episcopal chapel outside Jeffrey, in a clearing of ancient oaks, built years before the larger church on Main Street, used now only in summers for the eight o'clock service. The usual rector was vacationing in California. The summer priest said good morning. The worshipers responded good morning. The summer priest rattled off the prayers and collects. The readings sped by. Kate was having a hard time concentrating. She had worked her way from shoes to panty hose. Only when she knelt during the confession of sins did she put George momentarily out of mind.

Peace be with you, the priest said. The parishioners returned the greeting. George stood and shook hands with the people near him. He didn't seem nervous or self-conscious. He smiled warmly and sat down. The priest asked if there were any announcements. His eyes glanced around the congregation. He sensed everyone was looking at one person. He took up the look too, regarding George with curiosity and expectation, as if George might rise and address the congregation. He didn't, and the service continued.

When George's turn came, he knelt and received the bread and wine. Kate could see his footwear, blue socks and sandals with thick soles. She thought of the sandaled feet of the Apostles trekking across deserts. There was a spiritual aspect to George's character, everyone said so. Those sandals in the seventies made out of chunks of old car tires also came to mind. There was no place in that image for George.

George returned to his seat, bowed his head, and repeated the closing prayer. George sometimes attended church twice a week. Madge accompanied him a couple of Sundays a month. She was in Maine now visiting her sister, who had lupus.

Outside, the refreshment committee had set up a table by the stone wall. Hank usually headed home to change into his golf clothes. This morning he picked up a Dixie cup of juice.

George emerged from the church with Edith Runkle and her puppy, a guide dog in training. Edith kept tugging the leash to keep the puppy by her side. George bent down and let the dog lick his face. George was graceful the way he kept his legs together, Kate thought.

Whatever Edith wanted to say to George was taking a long time. She couldn't see very well. People joked the next dog was going to be hers. "Maybe she hasn't noticed the dress," Hank said into Kate's ear.

Certainly everyone else had noticed. Several walked by and patted George on the back or squeezed his arm, gestures that reminded Hank of how people comfort the bereaved at funerals when they want to be sincere but don't want to stop and actually say anything, except most of these people were trying not to smile. "Let's go," Hank said. He was tired of waiting. His tee time was in a hour.

"Why do anything?" Kate asked in the car on the way home.

"I think I deserve an explanation," Hank said. "I'm his attorney. What do you think?"

"I think he should have the dress taken in if he's going to wear it again."

"Come on, Kate. Be serious."

"I mean it."

"You really mean, leave George alone."

"That's right. He doesn't have to explain his choices to us."

By the time Hank arrived at the course, people in the clubhouse were already discussing George.

"Dress or no dress, he can't drive from the women's tees," someone said, and everyone laughed, except Hank.

Ronnie Gault, who had been at the service and agreed with Kate about the dress, said George should seek professional help, "a seamstress." Hank forced himself to smile.

Someone else suggested that Hank cross out the words "being of sound mind" from George's will. Hank turned away and headed for the door.

Recently George had changed his will. If Madge predeceased him, the half of George's estate that would have gone to Madge's sister would go Princeton and the other half to a cousin who lived in Connecticut. George and Madge had married late and didn't have children, two pieces of information that stuck in Hank's mind the rest of the morning.

There were usually other things on Hank's mind on summer Sunday mornings: golf, lunch, and after lunch. Kate would prepare pasta with fresh mushrooms, tomatoes, and local garlic; or salads with different homegrown lettuces and spinach, topped with chicken or shrimp. Hank would open a bottle of wine. There would be bread and cheese to nibble with the last of the wine, and later Hank and Kate would curl up on the day bed on the sunporch and make love and fall asleep.

When Kate woke up, Hank was staring at the ceiling.

"I'm thinking about George," he said.

"You figured him out yet?"

"I was thinking I really don't know him very well. He was fifty when he moved here and married Madge. No kids, of course."

"You're wondering what he did before he moved here?"

"Among other things."

"Such as?"

"Why did he marry Madge?"

"No, you're wondering what kind of marriage they have."

"Okay. What kind of marriage do they have?"

"Compatible, I'd say. They both like music. They both like to travel. They both like sailing. They read a lot. They're both good dancers."

"He still owns an apartment in Boston."

"So, it's convenient for them to use when they go to Boston."

"George goes by himself too."

"You're saying he has a secret life?"

"George is very elegant. I've never thought Madge was."

"You mean you don't understand how George could be physically attracted to Madge?"

"Is he? Does Madge ever say what they do together?"

"No, but I've never told her what we do."

"But other women tell you things. You tell each other things."

"We have ways of passing information to each other, intimate information, comrade." Kate's voice sounded like that Russian spy's in Rocky and Bullwinkle episodes. Hank tried to remember her name. Natasha, maybe.

"People used to make marriages of convenience all the time."

"There's a phrase I haven't heard for a while," Kate said.

"That doesn't mean they don't exist anymore."

"Are you saying George is gay?"

"I'm not saying that."

"But you've considered it?"

"Briefly."

"A transvestite?"

"Briefly."

"What are you considering now?"

"I've given up."

"Let's work from the other direction," Kate said. "Let's believe George is passionately, madly in love with Madge. In every way. On a summer night when their windows are open, you can hear their joyful noises. But they spend too much time apart. Madge's sister has lupus. She's dying. After she dies, Madge is going to be deeply unhappy. She'll live by herself in her sister's house, cleaning up, sorting out, remembering, mourning. George is going to be very alone. It will be as if Madge has died too. He knows that already. He feels it in the worst way. He gets up one morning to go to church. He sees the dress on the hanger. He smells Madge's smell. He puts on the dress. He puts Madge on. He walks out of the house in the dress."

"That's a nice story," Hank said. "Sad but nice."

"I like it too," she said.

She rested her head on Hank's shoulder. They didn't say anything for a while.

"I took a pair of your underwear once."

"When?"

"You were on your Italian trip with the other women. You were gone a long time."

"Three weeks."

"I missed you. I was desperate."

"Did you wear them?"

"I'm too big."

For a moment Kate pictured Hank naked, sorrowful, holding in his hands her underwear that won't fit him.

"I folded them up and kept them in my pocket. I just touched them sometimes, pretending I was touching you," Hank said.

Kate leaned over and kissed him. "I'm glad you told me," she said.

She lay back down beside him and closed her eyes. She could already feel his regret. He told her too much. He had been desperate. Her story about George reminded him. Then she thought, he's been down this road before, hasn't he? His own version, anyway. In his imagination, I died. A random act of violence, the wrong place, the wrong time? Was I gunned down? Or was I ill? Did I have a terminal disease? Flying somewhere, did my plane crash?

The questions stopped. She said to herself, *How* doesn't matter, does it? *How* isn't the point.

A few minutes later, Hank got of bed. She opened her eyes. He didn't turn around. Kate didn't see his face. The bathroom door closed. He wanted his privacy back. So did she. He would come out dressed in familiar clothes. He and Kate would go about the rest of the day as if nothing had happened.

∽ C WORDS ∽

When Cissy's mother attended Shippen College, in Jeffrey, the school was all girls and the interstate hadn't been built yet. Dartmouth was the nearest men's college. Slippery bus rides on the narrow New Hampshire roads brought Shippen women from Jeffrey to Hanover for winter parties. Men encircled the bus, cheering or giving a boisterous thumbs-down to the faces in the frozen windows. Eventually Cissy's mother married a Dartmouth man and moved to Texas, a state she learned to get along with but never to love. She was deeply pleased when Cissy, who excelled at field hockey, elected to attend Shippen and not a southern school like Agnes Scott or Sophie Newcomb.

Cissy met and married a Dartmouth man too, Spud Pringle. The Pringle Insurance Agency had been writing policies in Jeffrey for a hundred years. Spud didn't have to work very hard to make an excellent living. The business ran itself, leaving Spud plenty of time for golf. Golf kept Spud in shape. At sixty, Spud and Cissy usually made love once a week. Whether we want to or not, Spud joked to others in their social circle, well-off people who faced the physical diminutions of the aging process with cocktails and edgy, revealing humor. Spud, Cissy thought, received the gentleman's grade of C in almost everything, including making love. But *c* was the first letter in *comfort*. She loved comfort most of all.

Summers in Jeffrey were particularly comfortable when Spud played well. He had spent March and April in Florida getting a head start on the season. He was determined to win the senior championship at his club. Three times he had been runner-up.

"Do you remember someone named Myron Ackley?" Spud asked.

It was eight o'clock and the warmth of the day lingered into evening. Spud had grilled steaks, sipping his vodka and telling Cissy about making five birdies on the back nine that afternoon.

Cissy shook her head. "He remembers you," Spud continued. "His father worked at the college."

"I remember Dr. Ackley. He taught French."

"What do you remember about him?"

"He was tall and thin." She tried to think what else. "He had an affair with Arlene Givens."

"Really?" Spud smiled and filled Cissy's wineglass with the red he had bought that afternoon on the recommendation of one of his foursome. He topped off his own glass and speared his last bite of steak. While he chewed, he stared over Cissy head. She wasn't sure if he was looking at her or at the mountain behind her in the distance. He swallowed and smiled again.

"Myron was in my high school class," he said.

"Then why are you asking me?"

"I was curious how he knew you."

"You said he remembered me."

"Same thing, isn't it?"

"Well, I don't remember him. Maybe he dated someone at the college who knew me."

"The year he got kicked out," Spud said.

"Out of what?"

"Out of Yale. They let him back in, though. He was a nerdy science kid. A lab rat. He teaches science at the high school."

Spud had gone to high school in Jeffrey. Now the Jeffrey students attend the regional school built near the country club, between Jeffrey and Sutton. Cissy's mother's house had been in Sutton.

"There must be a point to all this," Cissy said. She had kicked off her shoes and was caressing Spud's foot with hers.

"There is. I've been watching Myron play golf. He's good. He's very good. In fact, he's too good."

Cissy leaned back and raised her face to the sky. "Nice breeze," she said. "It's giving me goose bumps." That was an invitation for Spud to rub her arms. The chill was affecting her nipples too. She hoped Spud would investigate.

"Myron fools you. See him in the market and he's the same old nerd. Remember Mr. Boynton, the biology teacher on *Our Miss Brooks*?"

"I remember *Mr. Peepers*."

"Boynton was taller than Peepers, not as frail. Then you see Myron with a club in his hand and you think he's a different person. Like in the clubhouse he took off one Myron and put on another."

"Super Myron."

"Yeah. Super Myron."

"Was Boynton gay?"

"I don't know. Peepers was, wasn't he?"

"I think the actor was. Wally Cox?"

"Maybe. Who knows? Who cares?"

"What about Myron?"

"First month at Yale he had a woman in his room all night. We couldn't believe it. In high school Myron couldn't get a date. Girls laughed at him. He told the dean he and this girl were discussing atomic something-or-others and lost track of time. She tried to sneak out in the morning. The dean didn't buy it."

Cissy was sliding her hands over her thighs. Spud wasn't buying anything either, certainly not the message she was sending. He stood up, fixed his attention at a spot on the ground, and guided his arms back and forth as if he held a putter. Putting was the weak part of Spud's game. He felt by himself on the fairways, relaxed. On the greens the game grew small and personal. Spud didn't like people watching him. Maybe he couldn't figure out what was on Cissy's mind, but she could read his. He was worried about Myron.

"How's Myron on the greens?" Cissy asked.

"Perfection," Spud said.

Later, in bed, Spud quickly fell asleep. Not Cissy. She regretted saying anything about Arlene Givens. Arlene was in her late sixties. She looked much younger, flirted outrageously, and sold as much real estate as any other agent in town. Her affairs with a couple of the businessmen in Jeffrey Spud probably knew about. Not Dr. Ackley, though. Arlene had been young then. Dr. Ackley was twice her age. Only Cissy and Yvonne and Betsy, her roommates, knew what was going on. One autumn afternoon Betsy had discovered Dr. Ackley and Arlene in the woods. They were both naked. They stood in a stream and she washed him, washed his "you know," Betsy said. "Penis," Yvonne said. "Cock," Cissy said. "He's so big," Betsy said, measuring with her hand, thumb and forefinger spread apart.

The roommates never told anyone else. They invented the Ackley scale, ten being tops. The roommates would point to the men surrounding the bus and do some evaluating of their own: three fingers, four. Sometimes a five. Spud was a five. Although she hadn't been with a lot of men, five was average in her experience. Perhaps Armand, the graduate student she'd slept with when she commuted to a summer program at Tufts, was a six. A summer in the past, the time Tommy, her son, was sixteen and worked at one of the summer camps on the lake.

Monday morning. Cissy pushed her cart and studied the other shoppers in Vivaldi's market with renewed interest. Maybe she'd see this Myron, in his nerd form. She looked for someone resembling his father. The only man about the right age weighed two hundred pounds, biceps the size of grapefruits. Not bad, but not Myron.

In the car, Cissy asked herself, Why am I interested? Why do I care about Myron? She answered, Because he remembers me and I don't know who he is. Do I want him to remember me? she continued. Do I like being in his mind? What's it like in there?

At home again, she put on her glasses and opened the phone book. She balanced the name on the tip of her red fingernail. M. Ackley, Lake Road, Sutton. Her mother had lived on Lake Road. The coincidence offered encouragement.

At the public library Cissy found Arlene returning an armful of videos. Another encouraging coincidence. Arlene suggested lunch.

At noon the taproom at the inn was crowded with summer people.

"My competition will tell you I make all my deals in here. That's not true. It's only the ones I care about," Arlene said, leaving Cissy to conclude that Arlene, true to her reputation, wasn't talking about real estate. Arlene ordered a lobster roll and a Zinfandel. Cissy ordered iced tea and chicken salad.

"Arlene, I want to apologize for something I said about you the other night. Spud asked if I knew Myron Ackley. I said I didn't, but I remembered his father.

For some reason I mentioned you and Dr. Ackley. Blame it on the wine we were drinking. I'm really sorry."

"I thought I'd kept that one a secret."

"One of my roommates saw the two of you in the woods."

"He was a sweet man. And hung like a stallion."

"That was reported too."

"I don't know Myron very well. He's a teacher. A couple of years ago he got interested in golf. He even went to golf school. "

"Spud said he's good."

"I don't play, so I don't understand how much of the game is skill and how much is luck, but I've heard Myron is so consistent that luck's not an issue with him."

"Does he resemble his father?"

"Honey, keep in mind I don't have the same familiarity with the son as I did with the father, but generally yes. Myron's sort of a beanpole like his dad."

"I don't think I've ever seen him."

"In the summer, if he's not playing golf, he comes into the library at nine every Thursday, when the new titles go on the shelf."

Thursday morning it rained. From the computer room, Cissy could observe him without his seeing her. His green rain jacket dripped on the carpet in front of the nonfiction shelves. His skin was smooth and tan. He had thin fingers and wrists, black hair, and gray sideburns. He moved to the fiction shelves. Mostly mysteries and romances. He wasn't interested in those. He turned away. She stood by the window and watched him cross the street. His Saab was parked near the bank. A blue sedan, about five years old. Cissy wondered if Myron was married.

"Myron's never been married," Spud said. "There was a lady attorney who practiced in Concord. She stayed for a while. But no one now. No one to distract him from his game."

"Do I distract you?"

"Only in good ways," Spud answered.

Cissy lay in Spud's arms. She could detect what dots his brain waves were connecting. He was on the eighteenth green and needed to sink the putt to win. The pro in Florida had told him to visualize, to see himself making the putt before he struck the ball. But Cissy knew he was seeing Myron's ball going in.

During the next week Cissy could feel the comfortable rhythm of the summer going out of tune. Anyone could enter the club championship. Any golfer in the state might show up, but Spud wasn't worried about any golfer, only Myron. Spud said, "Myron never has a bad day."

In their marriage, Cissy and Spud avoided guilt. Without any discussion, which would have seemed self-conscious and suspect, as if they were trying to defend the indefensible, they agreed vows of fidelity applied to the mind or spirit or soul, but not the body. They also believed in discretion and consideration and privacy. Armand had lived in Massachusetts. The afternoons with him in Boston at the Somerset were neither indiscreet nor inconsiderate. As the light dimmed beyond the drawn shades, Cissy felt refreshed, her soul restored, her body eager to return to Spud. In fact Spud had been the one to suggest that she might enjoy escaping the routines of Jeffrey by taking a course in something that interested her. She had enrolled in masterpieces of French literature in translation.

Another rainy day. Myron saw a woman standing in his yard looking at the lake. The air was so misty he could hardly see more than the woman and the shore. She wore a sweater but no jacket. Her hair hung straight and wet. Myron heated some water and walked out the back door to ask if he could offer her something hot to drink.

"Tea would be nice," Cissy said.

"You're . . ."

"Cissy. I guess you knew that." She held out her hand. Both of their hands were wet now. "My mother lived down the street." Cissy nodded toward the houses beyond some hemlocks.

"So you're not lost."

"Is that what you thought?"

"You looked lost."

"Just thoughtful."

She followed him inside. An A-frame. Each floor was one large room. Living area downstairs. Sleeping area upstairs. Sliding glass doors. Teak furniture. Bright rugs. She wondered what the bedroom looked like. Myron handed her a towel to dry her hair.

"Tea green or black?"

"Green."

"Strong or weak?"

"In between."

"Milk, lemon, sugar?"

"Nothing."

The steam from her mug warmed her face.

"You told Spud you remember me."

"After Yale gave me time off for bad behavior, I drove the coach."

"The coach?"

"The company called it a coach. You riders called it a bus."

"The one to Dartmouth, you mean? We called it lots of things."

"I don't think you had a good time. You cried on the way home. I wanted to kiss you."

Cissy sipped her tea. In this dialogue, her next line was obvious, but the timing was tricky. Cissy counted four beats.

"Do you want to kiss me now?"

"Yes, but I'm not going to."

"Do you want to kiss me because you think I'm still unhappy?"

"On the contrary. I think you're very happy with Spud."

"So Spud's why you're not going to kiss me?"

"Do you want me to kiss you?"

"I wouldn't mind."

Myron kissed her. She held out her arm trying to keep the tea from spilling. His mouth excited her. She put down her tea and kissed him back. They leaned against the counter and kissed for several minutes, their mouths wet, their bodies pushed together.

"Let's leave this at kissing right now," Cissy said.

Her tea had cooled, but she carried the mug to the sliding door. The sky was dark enough for them to see their reflections.

"You've remembered me for a long time," Cissy said.

"The way a frog remember a princess."

"You were a frog?"

"I'd say that."

"Is that what the woman in your room at Yale thought?"

"Probably. She was there because I paid her. She asked me something and my answer bored her so much she fell asleep. I was too timid to wake her."

"When did you outgrow being a frog?"

"In graduate school."

"Another professional?"

"A microbiologist. A rainy summer afternoon. Like today. And lots of tequila."

"You didn't offer me any."

"You don't like tequila."

"How do you know?"

"You mentioned it on the bus. You said, I don't like tequila and it's time to go home."

"I have a car now, but I stand by the rest of my statement."

"Will you come back sometime?"

"I liked kissing you, but I think you have something else in mind."

"So do you," he said.

Cissy's cheeks warmed.

"Did you go to mind-reading school too?"

"In a way I did."

"What's your reading now?"

"What's yours?"

"You think you haven't completely stopped being a frog," she said.

Spud slept. Cissy lay awake. Years ago, a melancholy young man had driven the bus she was on. She had been melancholy too. He had never forgotten her. In some turgid drama, they would meet again. Chords would swell the air. Seas would pound the shore . . .

Another story was playing in Cissy's head. The trick would be to make a deal without disturbing his tender memory of the girl on his bus.

Thursday was sunny. Myron phoned around eleven. Spud would be on the course until five.

"The coach leaves at noon," Myron said. "There's an empty seat."

Myron had set the picnic table by the lake with straw mats and green napkins. The tableware had matching green handles. He had arranged blue flowers in a beaker of water. Tiny bubbles floated up from the stems.

"I know you like quiche," he said. That told her all she needed to know.

Myron set out tomato salad to go with the quiche, which he admitted buying at a café in Concord. The wine he poured was light and dry. He saw Cissy looking at the plates. They were different colors.

"Mix and match. I go to lots of yard sales."

"Fiesta," Cissy said.

Myron didn't understand.

"It's called Fiestaware. People collect it."

"I like bright things," Myron said. "I like the dress you're wearing."

Cissy had put on an orange sundress the color of poppies.

They ate slowly, gazing at each other with anticipation. He refilled their glasses. He kissed her. He pressed his hand between her throat and her breasts. His touch tingled down her body.

Myron conducted Cissy upstairs. He undressed her. She was the same girl she was on the bus, he said. Just as lovely. Just as beautiful. When he stepped out of his own clothes, Cissy's eyes widened. Like father, like son.

He took his time, touching her all over, discovering what she responded to, trying to please her. He succeeded.

"I feel I've just gone back and lived part of my life again," he said. "And this time I wasn't a frog."

She was lying under the sheet. He was sitting on the side of the bed. He stroked her thigh.

"How did you get so good at golf?" Cissy asked

"Golf always looked easy to me. The club applies force to the ball. The ball has a certain shape and responds in certain ways. You need to learn to apply force to the ball the same way every time in every situation."

"Why are you better than Spud?"

"He's picked up too many bad habits."

"Anything else?"

"He's too much of a gentleman. When the pressure's on, he backs away, as if he doesn't care about winning. But he really cares too much. His body reads the confusion and starts doing things differently. Then there goes his game."

"Don't you care about winning?"

"I like to win, but I'm not afraid to lose."

"So it wouldn't hurt you to lose to him?"

Myron continued to stroke her thigh. For a while he didn't say anything, only smiled in a bemused way. Finally he said, "You led up to that nicely. What makes you think it's going to be him and me playing for the championship?"

"Because he's visualized it. He sees it happening, so it's going to happen. Isn't that the way visualization works?"

"You're taking it to a different level."

"What about us? What level are we on?"

"I liked this afternoon. Will you come again?"

Cissy laughed. "I don't have time right now."

Myron laughed too. "You know what I mean."

"Next Thursday, I promise," Cissy said.

At home Cissy showered and put on fresh clothes. Spud was irritable. Usually he would sip his drink, watch the evening fill up the yard, talk about his day, listen to Cissy talk about hers.

"I expected to see Super Myron on the course today. Probably too busy for us. Tiger Woods wanted some pointers."

Cissy stood behind Spud and massaged his shoulders. "You need to relax," she said.

"You're right. What did you do today?"

"Drove around and did some antiquing."

"Buy anything?"

"Made an offer."

"On what?"

"Not saying. It's a surprise."

The following Thursday Cissy packed some sandwiches and fruit in a picnic basket and drove to Myron's. The day was cool for early August. Myron had put a vase of yellow lilies on the table and turned down the bed.

Laundry soap made the fresh white sheets smell woodsy and autumnal.

Myron wasn't as tender this time. He didn't kiss and explore, touch and hesitate. He did the things that pleased her before. Some men watched the clock. Myron seemed to be following a schedule, or a protocol, as one duplicating an experiment might do, hoping to achieve the same results twice. Because Cissy's pleasure was the desired result, she didn't object. The outcome was more than satisfactory.

Later, her head resting on Myron's shoulder, the air feeling like a cool cloud on her skin, she asked once more about losing to Spud.

"I'm going to beat him," Myron said.

Not the answer she expected. It was what a frog would say. She knew about frogs.

Years ago Bertie Deever, a ventriloquist, performed all over the world. She had been a friend of one of the former presidents of the college, long dead now, which was why she came to Jeffrey in the first place. She stayed on because she was tired of traveling. Cissy had once asked Bertie to perform at Hospital Day, but she declined. She lived in a tiny house outside of town. Sometimes Cissy saw her sitting in a chair under a pear tree in her yard. Cissy would stop and talk. She guessed she was the only person who remembered what Bertie had been famous for.

Cissy offered her a hundred dollars. This time she accepted. You wanted me to do Hospital Day for nothing, she said. This is more important, Cissy replied.

On Monday Spud's team won the club scramble. He was in a good mood. The tournament began on Friday. Two days. Thirty-six holes. Handicaps were excluded from the scoring. Spectators usually gathered at the holes near the service road, where people could get out of their cars and watch.

Spud teed off early Friday. He played in a foursome of people he knew and felt comfortable with. Myron started later. Spud played well, especially his irons. He concentrated on his own game and gave little thought to what Myron might do, other than knowing he would do well. As Cissy predicted, Spud's hardest holes were the seventh, the ninth, the fifteenth, and the eighteenth, the ones near the road.

Not many spectators came out the first day. Saturday would be different. Spud's round was two over par. He was home taking a shower when the director called to tell Spud that Myron was one over. In the draw Spud and Myron would be playing in the same foursome Saturday. Just the way I saw it happening, Spud said at dinner.

A bright, warm morning. Bertie, wearing a tweed skirt, a white blouse the color of her hair under her straw hat, and beige tennis shoes, rode with Cissy to the seventh hole. Count on me, she said and got out first, joining the other spectators. Cissy waited a few minutes then got out too.

A man carrying a walkie-talkie wiped the leader board with a towel and updated the scores. Now Spud was three over. Myron was even par. The next best score was five over.

Cissy shaded her eyes and saw Spud and Myron. Spud was on the edge of the fairway, Myron in the center and closer to the green. Spud's iron shot rolled to the edge of the green. People applauded. Myron's dropped his ball ten feet from the cup. More applause.

Hank Tweed and Marty Benson, the other members of the foursome, needed another shot to reach the green. They marked their spots. Spud putted first. In the hush Cissy heard the tap of the club against the ball. The ball curved in a weave of grass and stopped on the lip, then dropped in.

The spectators grew silent again. Myron took his time settling over his ball. He stroked it. "*Ribbit*," croaked a very loud bullfrog. Frog? People looked at each other, looked at the ground trying to find the noisemaker. So did Myron. He wasn't watching when his ball fell into the hole.

Later Spud would say, "You could see from Myron's face how confused he was."

As the foursome approached the ninth green, the man corrected the leader board. Spud had gained a stroke. Myron stood aside waiting for the others to finish putting. He studied the ground and swung his club back and forth, as if concentrating, but Cissy knew he was thinking about frogs. Spud sank a nice twelve-footer to par the hole. Myron struck his own ball. "*Ribbit*," croaked the loud frog. Myron turned angrily toward the spectators, who were grinning at one another. Myron's putt stopped an inch short of the cup. He tapped in, losing a stroke.

"He tensed up just as he stroked the ball. I'd never seen him do that before," Spud would say.

Spud was down one coming to the fifteenth. This time Myron's ball was away. He positioned himself to putt, but stopped and scanned the crowd, which was larger now. The man with the walkie-talkie hushed them. Myron bent over his ball again. Cissy saw that Hank Tweed and Marty Benson had their eyes on the crowd too. So did the walkie-talkie man.

As soon as Myron's club met the ball, "*ribbit*" spoiled the silence. Most of the crowd tittered. Instead of watching his ball, Myron's eyes followed the walkie-talkie man. He pushed through the crowd and grabbed the arm of a spectator standing next to Bertie. She insisted the man had never uttered a word. The walkie-talkie man apologized.

Myron's putt stopped fifteen inches from the cup. When the hole was finished, Myron and Spud were tied.

"Hank and Marty couldn't tell who was making the sound either," Spud said. He was leaning back in his chair and smiling. Through the window he could see his trophy shining in the kitchen light. "The wind just seemed to go out of Myron's sails. When he teed off on the sixteenth, he shrunk down like he wanted to be invisible."

Spud led by one stroke at the eighteenth. Myron putted. Bertie didn't make a sound. She didn't have to. Myron was so angry he snarled *ribbit* himself, as if he was cursing the ball or the crowd or himself. Some spectators snickered; others, embarrassed, pretended they hadn't heard anything.

Myron bogeyed the hole and finished four over. Spud was two strokes better.

"When we shook hands, he looked awful. I almost felt sorry for him," Spud said.

Then Spud smiled. "*Ribbit*," he said and laughed. "Who was doing that? Have any idea?"

"None," Cissy said.

A few days later Cissy encountered Myron at Vivaldi's filling a shopping cart with Red Baron pizzas.

"I prefer Celeste," Cissy said. "By the way, where did you get the idea I like quiche? I don't. But Spud thinks I do."

"He mentioned it," Myron said.

Of course Cissy had understood that, had counted on it. But whatever Spud and Myron had discussed didn't matter. They couldn't have planned what happened. "What happened was my idea," Cissy said.

"I know," Myron said.

Did he know what she was thinking: He was still a frog, but a perfect ten?

"You'll probably win next year," she said in a low voice of condolence. She started to push her cart into the aisle.

"It's not Spud's game I'm worried about, it's yours," Myron said. She turned around.

"Maybe Spud won't enter."

"He has to. He's the champion."

"Some men know when to quit."

"Some women don't," Myron answered.

"What are you trying to say?" Cissy asked.

"You're driving the bus now. You're in control. It's going to be your call."

Myron held open the freezer door. Chilly air spilled into the aisle. People going by glanced at them, then looked away. Cissy thought Spud was there too. He was waving his arms to stop her, to bring her back.

"If there's an empty seat, I'll let you know," she said, trying to sound collected, playing along with his metaphor, as if Myron's words meant nothing concrete, nothing she should take seriously.

"There'll be one. I'm sure of it," he said.

Much to Cissy's confusion, she knew there would be one too.

~ CHANGING LIGHT ~

Lenny loved driving stoned. The evening sky hovered over velvet water, the water shimmered into a purple field. He could run across it to the other side of the lake without falling in. The cottage where the highway turned at the end of the lake blazed in orange fire.

Lenny negotiated the change of direction as he drove past the cottage up the hill to Laura's house. She nestled beside him, her heels on the cracked vinyl dash of the Fairlane. Two years ago, when he turned sixteen, the car had been Lenny's birthday present. Lenny and Laura had spent this day hanging out in Woodstock, examining the cars of the tourists who browsed the craft shops and galleries. Lenny had liberated a concealed twenty-dollar bill from the console of a silver Bravada, along with some tokens he could use at the tollbooth on the way to Manchester, where his mother lived.

Lenny spent ten of the stolen twenty on gas. He also bought a dozen doughnuts, coffee for himself, and a soda for Laura. They sat on a boulder above the river and ate the doughnuts and snickered at the fishermen in waders slipping on the wet stones. When Laura finished her soda, she lit a cigarette from the pack she'd scooped up from the seat of a red Bonneville with the license plate SMOKE ME. Why not? She leaned against Lenny and exhaled, letting him slip his hand under her Rolling Stones shirt, which had cost her fifty cents at the Jeffrey thrift shop across the street from the Mobil station, near the corner where Main Street divided. Lenny's father owned the station.

Dr. Ripley, Laura's father, was a dentist. He had inherited the lake frontage and the cottage whose tin roof was darkly radiant to Lenny's eyes looking down from the porch of Laura's house. She had gone inside to check for her parents. Her father usually worked late and liked to drink Dewar's at the inn before driving home. Laura's mother was a trauma nurse at the hospital in Hanover. Laura suspected she was having an affair with one of the doctors.

"No one here," Laura said. "Want to come in?"

"Hold on," Lenny replied. Dope tended to diminish his erotic inclinations. He continued to stare at the cottage. When the weather broke in May, Dr. Ripley had hired Lenny to help paint the clapboards red. As Lenny watched, a Jaguar sedan eased into the side yard of the cottage. A man and a woman stepped out.

"Dad rented them the cottage the rest of the month," Laura said, standing beside Lenny as the cottage lights blinked on one by one.

"Tomorrow. Okay?" Lenny sounded distracted.

Okay with Laura. She didn't mind having sex in Lenny's car. She did mind doing it in her room. Lenny got a buzz from the chance one of her parents might catch them. She didn't. Anyway, she preferred just kissing and holding Lenny close to her.

Lenny maneuvered the Fairlane down the hill. The man was lifting suitcases from the trunk of the Jaguar. Leather ones. A matched set. No nylon zip-ups from Penney's like the bag his father gave him for the senior bus trip to Washington. Lenny wondered if the luggage hid anything small and expensive.

Nolan Stout, Lenny's father, was going over accounts at the kitchen table. "I saved you a chop," he said. "There's iced tea and fresh corn."

Lenny took the plate off the warmer and poured his tea into a plastic tumbler, adding three teaspoons of sugar and watching it submerge in cloudy lines.

"You'd like Merrimack Tech," Nolan said.

Lenny shrugged. He was cruising the interstate in the Jaguar, taking the curves at ninety. Hardly a vibration.

"You need to notify them by September."

September. Two weeks away. The papers were full of back-to-school ads. Lenny read them and watched the colors run together. Laura was a senior this year. She had already gone a half day and picked up her schedule and books.

"Can't you use me around the station?"

"Now, but not after the summer people leave. You know the economy here. How come you didn't show up today?"

"I needed to hang out."

"With Laura?"

"Who else?"

"You see a future with her?"

"What's wrong with the present?"

Nolan shuffled the receipts and tried to concentrate on his account book. "You disappoint me," he said.

"Why?"

"You have to have a plan. You have to focus."

"You plan to get back with Mom?"

Nolan pushed the papers aside. "You got a mouth, you know that?"

"That's what Laura says."

Nolan removed his glasses, set them on the table, folded his hands, and watched Lenny eat. Lenny finished his meal and left his plate in the sink. He turned on the TV. The Red Sox were playing. "Hey, Dad, your team is losing again," Lenny announced.

Kim, Laura's mother, had the morning off and took Laura shopping at the mall close to the hospital where she worked. The point wasn't to buy anything, Laura knew. Shopping gave her mother an opportunity to ask Laura certain questions and make them seem offhand and casual. "Are your bras comfortable?" Kim asked at the lingerie counter, trying to find out why Laura had stopped wearing them. "Do you like this color?" Kim inquired, pointing to some cotton Jockeys, wondering why Laura had washed her own underpants all summer.

After coaxing Laura into accepting a skirt and sweater, Kim bought Laura lunch at a café outside the Dartmouth theater. Kim and the man at the next table looked at each other a lot. On the way home Laura commented that the man had an interesting face. "Maybe he's an actor," Laura said. "Or a doctor," she added, speaking quietly as if musing to herself. Kim knew Laura was asking her own questions. Kim pretended not to hear.

Lenny worked at the station until five. Then he skated down Main Street on his board past the bookstore and Laura's father's office. The station closed at six. Lenny returned in time to see the Jaguar stop in the full-service lane. He set the pump and wiped the windshield. The driver was sixty, Lenny guessed. His wife, about the same age. She wore a beige suit and sat with her legs crossed. She rested her hand on her knee. Her rings sparkled.

"Lenny . . ."

They were lying on Laura's bed, Lenny nuzzling her neck, his hands between her legs.

"Please stop. It's late."

Usually Lenny complained, but this time he sat up and glanced at the china clock on Laura's bureau.

"You're right," he said.

As Lenny walked down the hillside to the cottage, he moved in and out of shadows. He tried to see inside, but the curtains were closed. He approached the end of the porch that faced the road and the lake. The man rocked in a chair close to the railing, a newspaper open on his lap. His clothes caught Lenny's attention.

Lenny paused, then made his way around the rocks edging the bed of ferns in front of the porch. The woman sat on a chaise reading a book. Lenny noticed two glasses with long stems, a pitcher of ice, and some bottles on a lacquered tray. Lenny cleared his throat. The man raised his eyes. The paper rustled as he folded it.

"I'm Lenny." Lenny placed one foot hesitantly on the bottom step. "I helped Dr. Ripley paint this place. I came by to ask if you need anything."

"How very kind, but we're quite comfortable," the man said. He stood up and shook Lenny's hand. He wore a suit like the one Lenny rented for the prom, only his shirt was white, not powder blue, and his tie black. "Haven't I seen you before?"

"At the station," Lenny said.

Lenny's gaze moved up the woman's long white dress to her garnet necklace and matching earrings. Garnet was his birthstone, Lenny's mother had told him. The woman stared at Lenny until he withdrew his foot from the step. Then she smiled.

At least the people could have introduced themselves, Lenny mumbled to himself as he stalked up the hill until his muscles ached.

Later the sight of the couple on the porch in evening clothes surprised Dr. Ripley on his way home.

He drove by very slowly, keeping them in view as long as he could. They were sitting at a table, which they'd covered with a white cloth, eating dinner by candlelight. Kim liked to do that, he remembered.

The next day the man stopped at the station for a map. When he saw the golf trophies on the shelf above the cash register, he asked Mr. Stout's advice about local courses. Mr. Stout recommended Eastman and phoned to arrange a tee time.

At one o'clock Lenny parked where he could watch the cottage. His lucky day, since she played too. The couple stowed their clubs in the trunk of the Jaguar and drove off

Lenny knew where Dr. Ripley kept extra keys. He didn't need one, though. The cottage was unlocked.

Laura sat on a blanket sunning herself near the water. She saw Lenny climb the cottage steps and open the door. But he didn't go inside. He stood in the doorway. A few cars drove by, and she wished Lenny wouldn't stand where people could see him. For that matter, she wished he wouldn't take anything. He'd promised her earrings. Where would she wear them? No, she wished he'd leave things alone and lie beside her in the sunshine. She closed her eyes. Suddenly he was taking off his shirt and telling her to move over.

"What were you thinking?" she asked.

Lenny squeezed her hand hard. "I don't know," he said.

Coming home that night, Kim saw the man and the woman standing in the moonlight by the birch tree at the water's edge. His arm encircled her waist. She rested her head on his shoulder. Kim watched the couple for several minutes. She imagined she could hear their breathing. It was full of passion, wordless, but somehow it rhymed like lines in a sonnet.

All the next morning Lenny tried to figure out what had stopped him. The ticking of the ship's clock on the mantel? Wind rustling the curtains? The hum of the refrigerator? Something about the woman. Her smile? Yes, the smile he couldn't get out of his mind, her smug expression as she watched him lift his foot from the step and retreat to his own world. Lenny realized he'd been too angry to do anything other than leave again, go back to Laura on her blanket. The next time would be different.

Dr. Ripley stopped at the station before afternoon appointments and mentioned the candlelight dinner he'd witnessed on the cottage porch. After dark, Mr. Stout found himself wanting to take a drive, found himself driving around the lake, found himself parked off the road gazing at the couple on the porch too. They were dressed the way Dr. Ripley had described. They must be listening to some music playing inside the cottage that Mr. Stout couldn't hear because they stood up and started to dance, a slow step that reminded Mr. Stout of a time years ago when he had seen his father take his mother into his arms on a summer's night under the glow of Japanese lanterns.

Lenny skipped work again and watched the cottage until the couple appeared with a picnic basket and drove away.

The front door opened, no key needed. These people, did they think everyone here was honest? Did they believe pure air meant pure hearts? The way the question turned Lenny's attention to his own heart caught Lenny off guard. He wasn't used to asking such things, certainly not about himself.

The remarkable order surprised him. The couple had been there long enough to clutter the cottage, but their books were left neatly on the desk, their newspapers stacked on the table, their dishes put away, their clothes arranged in bureau drawers, their towels folded, their bed was made. Only the earrings beside the jewelry box on the dressing table seemed out of place. Lenny picked up the garnets and started to drop his hand to the pocket of his torn jeans. His heart throbbed. There wasn't enough air in the room to breathe. He stepped backward. The woman smiled again. But differently this time. A quizzical expression. Perhaps a bit of sadness. Even sympathy. The way his mother regarded him when they visited Boston and he forgot which subway car to take and had gone in the wrong direction.

Suddenly Lenny took a deep breath as if he had shot to the surface after a long time underwater. Space changed, the way it did sometimes when he smoked dope. But he hadn't smoked anything. He sucked the quiet into his lungs. For an instant he shed his skin like a wetsuit. He rose in the air and floated over the town. He saw everywhere, into every room. Everywhere he had ever been. He had been one Lenny, he had changed, he could change again. He opened the lid of the jewelry box and placed the earrings inside.

On Friday night Lenny invited Laura to a movie. Afterward, instead of parking in the woods off County Road and fooling around in the car, he drove Laura home. He dimmed his lights and coasted by the cottage. The couple in their evening clothes stood by the shore. The man appeared to be holding out his arms, like one casting a spell over sky, over trees, over water.

"You're back early," Mr. Stout said when he heard Lenny close the door.

"I guess so," Lenny answered.

Lenny went into his room, undressed, and hung up his clothes. In the morning he would tell his father he was going to Merrimack Tech. Maybe his father would phone his mother and tell her. The leaves would be changing soon. Maybe his father would invite her for a picnic. Or maybe his father and his mother would hike up Mount Blue and see below them the streets and tiny houses of the town disappearing in the enormous, changing light.

~ BONES ~

Carleton likes to drink at the Corners. He prefers the table under the bear's head. If he sat at the bar, he'd have to listen to Dokey complain about the Red Sox or the Bruins, depending on the season, or politicians. Unlike the rest of us, Dokey never complains about the weather. He'll tell you the weather's always okey-dokey with him. He expects you to smile. The real reason Carleton prefers a table is because either Molly or Cheryl will bring him his drink.

Dokey is from Montana. He was stationed in Portsmouth once. When his enlistment was up, he headed west. He wrecked his motorcycle avoiding a moose on the interstate. Jeffrey is as far west as he made it. Like any true bartender, he knows the value of memories. He didn't really want to go back to Montana. He concludes that fate took a hand and made its point the hard way.

Molly and Cheryl wear short flaring skirts, black stockings, boots, and shirts with fringe on the sleeves. When they turn around their skirts lift a little. More draft, he tells Molly when she takes away his empty glass. No pun intended, he adds. Molly gives him her "you're cute" smile. But Carleton knows she's thinking look all you want, old man, but don't touch.

I usually drink at the inn, mostly because Jimmy works there and it's across the street from my office. About once a month Carleton calls up and says to meet him. He used to be my father-in-law. He never asks about his daughter, whether she stuck with the man she went away with, whether or not she's happy. We discuss the same topics Dokey does, except we include the weather. And land. Carleton has land. The lake frontage, he's sold. He chooses his clothes at the thrift shop. He heats his three rooms with wood. He drives a Bronco old enough to buy a drink. His savings account pays less than three percent, but, as he says, three percent of a million isn't bad.

"What's up?" I asked.

Molly had just brought him a frosty glass and a plastic sombrero the size of an ashtray full of peanuts.

"I wish that lady's skirt was," he answered. He swallowed some beer and wiped his mouth with the back of his hand. "You ought to ask her out. Molly would be a good one."

"Good for what?"

"For what you need."

"Marriage, for instance?"

Carleton brushed stray Planters off the table. "Molly would be a good one for having children."

"I'm forty-four. I'm not ready for children."

"When was the last time you had dinner with a lady?"

"Last week."

"Mrs. Burns. I heard she let you drive her Caddie. I'm not asking about ladies older than I am who own properties you rent and you escort to the inn so they can have martinis and someone to drive them home."

"I know what you mean. I can't remember."

"You asked Molly?"

"No."

"Because she didn't finish high school? You realize, Rudy, you're sort of a snob."

"That's not the reason."

"Then why?"

"Carleton, you don't want to know."

"Ruin my illusions, would it?"

"It would."

"Go ahead."

"Molly's interested in someone else."

"Who?"

"Someone I did ask out."

The handful of Planters stopped halfway to Carleton's mouth. "Really?"

"That's what she told me."

"Molly told you?"

"The other lady told me."

The hand finished its journey. Carleton chewed and drank more beer. "That puts a whole new light on things, doesn't it?"

"Carleton, what's really on your mind?" I asked.

Carleton scooped up another fistful of Planters, frowning, as if giving serious consideration to what he going to say, and then he began a story that made me forget Molly and her friend and the fact that the Sox were blowing another game to Cleveland. Carleton tells me this: The maples in the marsh are already red. Carleton walks into the woods. He sees a couple of bears. The bears have flies buzzing around their heads. The bears don't bother him. Eventually he comes to a barn no one's used in a hundred years. The foundation stones are still there, the timbers fallen between them. He's studying the wood and wondering if lugging up the metal detector he bought at Sears would be worth the effort when he notices on the dark ground between two timbers what appears to be bone. A piece of bone. He pushes the wood away. Now he sees a whole leg, the bones of a human leg. He moves more wood. There's a skull, ribs, arm. The wrist still buried. He carefully replaces the timbers. He hasn't told anyone else what he's found.

"People building a new house near the lake uncovered Indian bones, but I don't think these are Indian bones," Carleton said.

"Better tell the deputy," I advised.

"I can't stand him. You went to college. You know any bone people?"

"Carleton, I studied psychology, not forensic anthropology."

"Is that what it's called?"

"I think so. Phone the deputy."

"He'll blab it around and I'll have a bunch of people up there."

"He won't. He'll tell a bone person."

"Psychology? I thought you took English. You read a lot."

"I have lots of free time."

"You read Havelock Ellis?"

"No. Have you?"

"Some."

"Learn anything?"

"We're all kooks."

"I won't blab it around."

"Maybe you and Molly and her friend could all get together."

"Carleton, you amaze me."

"You marrying my daughter amazed me."

"Why?"

"She's a free spirit. You're not."

"What about the bones?" I asked.

"What about them?"

"What do you think?"

"I think someone got killed. There was trauma to the skull."

"Trauma to the skull, that sounds official. You reading crime stories these days?"

"Havelock Ellis put me off reading. Made me an observer."

"And you observed what?"

"The skull had an extra hole in it, on the side where it shouldn't be."

"Then you should tell the deputy."

"I was hoping you knew someone, and we could find out something and not involve the police."

"You're not growing anything illegal, are you?"

"I wasn't before. Kids were. I got blamed because it was my land. If there's anything growing there or not, I don't know. But once with the deputy is enough."

"Carleton, you could leave the body where it is and not tell anyone."

"Wouldn't be right. Not knowing eats people up. Somewhere someone wants to find out."

Carleton was thinking about his friend Billy Proctor, who disappeared on a reconnaissance flight over the Pacific more than fifty years ago.

"Carleton, you have a theory, don't you?"

"Lots of them."

"I mean about the bones."

"I just wish you knew a bone person, that's all."

And that was all, all Carleton would say, other than to make a few more observations about Molly's body and the design of her skirt and the currents of air moving in the room. The next day he did tell the deputy, though. The deputy contacted the state police. One morning a team of men hiked to the barn. By evening the ground had been photographed, dug up and sifted, and the bones nestled in a van on its way to Concord.

The days were short now. The sun was precious. I ate my lunch outside my office and watched the cars go up and down Main Street. I could see the town hall and the cruisers in the parking lot. The summer people had gone. The leaf peepers were beginning to arrive, one or two cars at a time, not the busloads that would show up later. When I wasn't in the office, I was checking on my houses, making sure my crews were cleaning the rental units. I had two houses left to rent on the lake, both expensive. Leaf peepers weren't spending much this year.

Late one afternoon I was driving back from Concord and took the Warner exit. Warner is a few miles south of Jeffrey. It's the nearest town with a fast-food restaurant. The burger was cold, but the fries were warm. When I came out, the girl was standing by my car. Maybe she was twenty. Dark eyes and hair. She wore a Raiders jacket and jeans. The tarnished stripe on her running shoes matched her T-shirt. The thick soles of the shoes made her tall. Her hands were tiny, the nails, delicate as ladybugs, painted purple. She slid her hands into her jacket pockets and pulled back her arms. Her breasts pressed against her shirt. You take me to Jeffrey? she asked. I asked where. Bus stop, she said.

I bought her a chicken sandwich and some fries. She ate while I drove. When she finished she shook a cigarette from a pack of Marlboro's. My wife smoked. I enjoyed the way it made her mouth taste. In the morning I could still smell her breath on my skin.

"I like it here," the girl said.

"You like snow?"

"We have snow where I come from," she said. Then she leaned over and touched my leg with her hand. Fly away, fly away home, I thought, and wondered if that's what I really wanted. "I like lie in bed and watch snow fall," she said. I could hear Jimmy's voice too: Oh man, you better watch what you're thinking.

The afternoon bus from Boston stops at Jeffrey on its way to White River Junction. The café next to my office sells tickets. When the weather is warm, passengers sit at the tables outside and drink coffee and wait. I parked and pointed to my office. It was almost dark. The café was closed. If she was traveling to White River, I said, she'd have to buy a ticket on board. She regarded me sadly, as if I had said something wrong or used the wrong words. Maybe she was meeting someone. I said I was going to work in my office. She could knock on the door if she needed anything. Her mouth was soft and open, as if she might speak or wanted to be kissed.

A couple of other passengers were sitting at the tables. She walked over to them. From time to time I glanced out the window. She blended into the darkness with the others. When the bus came, I wasn't sure if I saw two people or three crossing the street. Anyway, they disappeared on the other side of the bus. The bus drove away. I closed the office and walked across the street. Carleton was looking for you, Jimmy said. I thought it was time Carleton heard something about the bones.

I was on my second drink when Carleton returned. The Sox were starting their last series of the year, playing out the season, letting some of the call-ups have a chance. Jimmy was explaining that even if the Red Sox had as much money as the Yankees, Boston still couldn't buy a winning team. Jimmy was preaching to the converted.

Jimmy poured Carleton a beer. We watched the game and finished our drinks. Carleton didn't say anything, which meant he had plenty to say. I paid the check. We stood in the parking lot. The moon was half full. A silvery light shone on the street where the bus stops.

"Here's what we know," Carleton said. "Eighty percent chance the bones belong to a man, probably Oriental, five feet five, more or less."

I wondered if one could say "bones belong to a man," as if they were merely possessions, things he could decide to leave or take with him wherever he went.

"Been dead at least fifty years, probably longer."

"And the wound?"

"Gunshot. Part of the bullet was stuck in the bone. Calcified, I think they called it. Probable cause of death."

"You did the right thing," I told him.

The comment seemed to catch Carleton off guard. He blinked and stared at me. "Maybe," he said. "Maybe not."

I assumed he was concerned about a story in the *Recorder,* Jeffrey's once-a-week newspaper. The bones made the Concord paper too, the same coverage: race, age, sex, and the evidence of a wound. Not many details were given about where the bones were found. Carleton's name wasn't mentioned. Reports of missing persons would be checked, what reports there were going back that far. If no one claimed the bones, the state would either bury them or keep them for forensic students.

I drove home and turned on the game. A Korean was pitching for the Sox. There was a Japanese player on the team too. At least a dozen students from Japan were enrolled at the college. But in 1950 or 1940, how many Asians lived in Jeffrey?

Bud Bryson owns the Texaco station. He's lived here all his life. He served in the Marines. Carleton had been a Seabee. Bud remembered a Japanese couple, a gardener and housekeeper at the Hoener estate. They left after Pearl Harbor, Bud said. Mrs. Tillson had a chauffeur who might have been Japanese. He went away too. I had never heard of Mrs. Tillson.

"Lived on Proctor Hill. Owned a Packard," Bud said. "Terrible driver. Good-looking woman. All the young bucks like me, Carleton, and Billy Proctor had it for Mrs. Tillson. Dark hair with some red in it. Pretty eyes. Played lots of tennis. Had a private court. We used to sneak over and watch. She wore those short tennis dresses. Forty maybe, but she didn't look it. Her husband was someone in Washington. He didn't stay here much. After the war, they divorced. She moved to California. He was killed in a plane crash."

"There's only one house on Proctor Hill," I said.

"The Tillsons' house burned down. People tried to pump water from the pond, but wasn't any use."

I walked back to my office thinking Carleton owned most of the land that used to belong to the Proctors. The woman was waiting at the door. Her white jacket and trousers looked like silk. She stood very straight. A round straw hat shaded her face.

"Are you Mr. Wheeler?" she asked. Her voice reminded me of the woman I had left at the bus stop. I wondered if they knew each other, or came from the same country.

The sun warmed my office. I offered to go next door and bring the lady coffee or a soda.

"Let us conduct our business first," she said. "My name is Wynn." She spelled it for me. "I wish to rent a house. The best, please."

"That would be on the lake," I said. "I have two to show you."

"You choose, Mr. Wheeler."

"How long will you need it?" I asked, then said, "Everyone calls me Rudy."

"A week perhaps."

"Peak foliage is a couple of weeks from now," I said.

"We have trees in my country too," she said.

"Mrs. Wynn . . ."

"Not Mrs. Wynn, just Wynn."

Her fingers were slender with a lovely shape. She wore a ring with a green stone on her right hand.

"Do you have a car?" I asked.

"I prefer not to drive," she said.

"The market isn't close. There aren't any restaurants nearby."

"Perhaps you can supply me a driver, then. I will pay more, of course. Or drive me yourself, if not inconvenient."

"Yes," I said, not knowing which option I was agreeing to.

I picked up the leather case she'd left by the door and walked to my car. The case didn't weigh much. Maybe she wore only silk. Maybe she could afford to. She settled into the seat. I pointed out the market, a restaurant, and the post office on our way to the lake, but she wasn't listening.

The house had been remodeled with tall windows and skylights. The furniture and the Berber carpet were also new. We stood on the deck. She put on sunglasses and took off her hat and unclasped her hair.

"Rudy, I would like some fruit," she said.

From June to October, Spring Meadow has fresher produce than the market. I returned with an assortment of peaches, plums, pears, bananas, apples, and a mango. "You did well," she said. "Would you suggest a place for dinner?"

"I suggest I pick you up at seven," I said. Where else was she going to find a driver?

I drove us up Proctor Hill to the old Proctor house, now named The Proctor and recently featured in *Dining* magazine. A couple from California had bought the place and turned it into a restaurant. The food is expensive, but locals receive a discount.

"I'm glad you have on a suit," Wynn said. "I prefer them on some men."

I thought I'd run that comment by Jimmy and see what he made of it. Wynn was in silk again, the red and yellow of the mango I had brought her. The long skirt was slit up the side, the matching jacket undone at the top. She wore no jewelry except the green ring, and no makeup except a delicate shade of red on her lips.

I drank two Johnny Walkers and tried to remember the balance in my checking account. She sipped a Veuve Cliquot cocktail and looked out the window. The forest comes up almost to the restaurant. I wondered what she was thinking, and if she could see anything in the dark.

We finished our drinks, ordered wine, and began to eat. I tried to be chatty but that didn't work. When she wasn't looking out the window she was looking at me. I looked back at her. Once I thought she blushed a little, as if she were reading my mind and didn't wholly object to my thoughts.

When I took her home, she stood at the door while I unlocked it. "I am very tired," she said. "But tomorrow I would like to walk. Where you took me tonight would be a good place to start," she said.

In the morning I stopped in town to deposit the check Wynn had given me for a week's rent. She carried no credit card, she explained. I asked the teller to phone my office if there was a problem. He gave me his your-problem-isn't-my-problem frown but promised he would.

"I will be fine," Wynn said after I suggested that her trousers, linen this time, sweater, cashmere I guessed, and sandals might not be the best outfit for a walk in the woods. Her tone told me it wasn't my place to make suggestions about her clothes.

We parked where we had the night before. I let her choose a path. She moved easily, gracefully, even when the path gave out. I stumbled over rocks and twisted roots trying to keep up. She found some rhododendrons and stopped.

"These do not grow here by themselves," she said.

There were lilacs too. A stone wall. A high fence entwined with creeper. The cracked remains of a tennis court. I searched among the weeds and found granite slabs on which a house had once stood. Past the fence, a pond, or what was left of it, mostly cattails now.

"Who lived here?" Wynn asked.

"I think a family named Tillson," I said.

She nodded, as if the name was familiar.

"There must be more," she said.

"I don't know much more than that," I said.

She gazed at me impatiently. "A garage. All Americans have automobiles, don't they?"

"Mrs. Tillson owned a Packard," I said.

Wynn nodded again. "Perhaps, like me, she preferred a driver?"

"I believe she did."

"Perhaps the driver—chauffeur isn't it?—lived upstairs above the Packard."

"I really don't know," I said.

"I know you don't *know,* but you are capable of imagining. When you looked at me last night, you had a very vivid imagination. What do you imagine about Mrs. Tillson and her chauffeur?"

"I think you have already imagined them better than I can."

Wynn smiled this time. "Good, Rudy. That is a good answer. You are right. I imagine a woman alone. Her husband is away frequently. He hired the driver himself. He wanted a competent man to drive his wife and take care of the Packard. Whom would he employ? All his choices involve prejudice, of course. Not a black man. The husband is aware of his wife's beauty. Black men are good drivers but they are too easily aroused and incapable of self-control. A white man? He will resent a woman telling him what to do. He will always tell her he can find himself another position and she will have to drive herself. An Asian man, a Japanese man, let's say. He is a commendable driver and admires machinery, keeps it in good condition. He needs employment. Though sometimes devious, he is loyal and respectful to superiors. His meager salary will seem a great amount to him. Now, Rudy, I know you can imagine what happens."

"She falls in love with him."

"Yes, I agree. They fall in love. If there are other servants, she dismisses them. The house is not so big she cannot manage it. She cooks. The tennis court? Perhaps the chauffeur tends its needs too. Or perhaps the gardener does. He works only a few hours a week. The wife and the chauffeur are mostly alone, except for one or two who arrive for tennis sometimes. But such tranquillity cannot last, can it?"

"The war."

"Yes, Rudy. The war."

I followed Wynn to the car. She said nothing. At the house, she said, "You will take me to dinner again, please?"

"What is the expression? 'Hang . . . hang out'? This is where you hang out?" she asked when I opened the door for her at the inn.

"At the bar," I answered.

"I do not object to sitting there with you," she said.

Jimmy gave me and my suit a quizzical look. He bowed when I introduced Wynn. "I want you to be happy tonight," she said to me. She ordered a martini. I saw Jimmy smile to himself as he turned away to pour our drinks. He brought my Johnny Walker rocks and Wynn's martini in a wide glass with a tall stem. She took a tortoise-shell case from her handbag and offered me a cigarette. "No thank you," I said. Jimmy lit hers with a Ronson lighter he'd bought at a flea market.

Jimmy asked if Wynn was from Japan.

"I have lived there, yes. And in other places. I am between countries now," she said.

"Sometimes I feel that way too," Jimmy said.

"You have an interesting hand," she remarked, admiring the tiny raised angel on Jimmy's signet ring.

"You know about angels?" Jimmy asked.

"Not very much," Wynn answered.

"You probably know more than I do," Jimmy said. "Do you believe in them?"

"I believe this one's kept me out of trouble."

The bar was filling up. We finished our drinks and went into the dining room to order.

"Opposites attract," I commented.

"That is a Western idea," Wynn said. "Who are you thinking about?"

"The chauffeur and Mrs. Tillson. He must have seemed very different to her."

"Perhaps kinder than her husband. More attentive. More devoted." Wynn paused, her eyes searching mine. "More ardent," she said.

I thought about telling Wynn that Mrs. Tillson's real chauffeur had gone away when the war started. But the imaginary one we were inventing was the only thing we talked about. I didn't want to give that up.

"Mrs. Tillson had to hide him," I said.

"Of course."

"Then something happened."

"Of course."

I imagined Carleton and his friends wending their way through the woods from Billy Proctor's house to spy on Mrs. Tillson, to watch her play tennis, a real beauty.

"Mr. Tillson found out," I said.

"Perhaps," Wynn answered.

I drove Wynn to the lake. "Would you care for a cup of tea?" she asked. I shook my head. "Then I hope to see you tomorrow," she said. She touched my sleeve, raised her mouth to mine, and kissed me lightly on the lips, a soft kiss I felt all the way home.

In the morning I was shopping for Wynn when Carleton saw me. "She's got you hoppin', hasn't she?"

"She?"

"Madame Butterfly."

"Her name is Wynn," I said.

"I didn't know you own a suit," Carleton said.

"You saw me get married in it."

"The deputy saw you bring her home. Said you didn't even turn off your lights."

"Is this any of your business?"

"What's her business?"

"I didn't ask."

"I think the bones brought her here."

"Carleton, be logical. How would she know anything? She's just a visitor renting a house."

"You know what they say about Orientals."

"Asians," I said.

"You're so damn politically correct, aren't you?"

"*Asians* is what they prefer."

"So you jump in line."

"Carleton, why are we having this conversation?"

"Because she's trying to tell you something and you're not getting it."

I opened my mouth to answer, but I didn't have anything to say.

I bought gas on the way to the office. I asked Bud if he was sure the chauffeur left town. Bud told me two things. First, Mrs. Tillson started driving herself and no one could forget the sight of the Packard going all over the road. Second, before Billy reported for service, he snuck over one more time to see Mrs. Tillson. She was playing singles with Mrs. Proctor. He wanted to take something of hers to keep with him for good luck when he shipped out. He went into the house. He wandered from room to room. There was nobody there. He opened up the closets and drawers. Looked all around. She lived there alone. No cook. No chauffeur. Not even her husband.

At the office I listened to my messages. The bank had phoned. The check was good. I drove to the lake with Wynn's fruit. She was dressed in pink silk slacks and a loose white blouse. She brewed a pot of tea and we sat on the deck. The lake was blue and empty. Wynn's cigarettes were on the table beside an open notebook.

"I work in the mornings," Wynn said.

I glanced at the notebook.

"You're a writer?"

Wynn glasses were very dark. I couldn't see her eyes. She leaned back in her chair and raised her face to the sun. Wynn wasn't wearing anything under her blouse. I thought of the girl who wanted a ride.

"I am someone a story is told through. This lake, Rudy, these mountains, these trees, the story starts with them. We must simply listen. The story we are imagining is already told. The forest has a version of it, stones have a version of it. We are simply passing on what's already there. You suggested the husband discovers the lovers. What happens next?"

"Do you know about the bones?" I asked. I told her what the papers had printed.

"My point exactly, Rudy. We are not making up something."

"The bones may not belong in our story at all."

"Let's assume they do."

Wynn's eyes questioned me. She waited for me to go on.

"The husband discovers his wife's feelings and kills the chauffeur," I said.

"What do you know about Mr. Tillson afterward?"

"He and Mrs. Tillson separated. She moved away. He died in an accident."

"Which leaves us to find out the chauffeur's name."

"We're assuming too much," I said. "We're putting together things that may not belong together."

"You need to put everything into categories and dimensions, don't you, Rudy? The dimension of the real, the dimension of the made up. You may as well try to separate the body and the spirit. Try to believe all things have presence in more than one dimension at the same time."

Wynn leaned on the railing and gazed across the water. "I know I'm boring you. You'd much rather make love to me."

I felt heat on my cheeks. "I didn't mean to make you uncomfortable," I said.

"You haven't. Though you've succeeded with yourself."

"Wynn . . ."

"Rudy, who discovered the bones?"

"Carleton LeMay. He used to be my father-in-law."

"Would he show me where?"

"Why?"

"So I could listen to what the earth says."

"Not if you put it that way."

"Perhaps he would tell you."

"He would know why I was asking."
"He knows about me already then?"
"He knows we've had dinner together."
"He doesn't approve?"
"Carleton is Carleton. He's moody."

At five in the afternoon Carleton was at the table under the bear's head. Dokey had wiped its eyes with oil. They appeared bright again. The yellow teeth would always be the same. Carleton's weren't much better.

I said I wanted to see where he'd found the bones.

"You're going show that Jap woman, aren't you?"

"I don't know if Wynn is Japanese or not," I answered.

"You can't tell one from another either, can you?"

"Carleton, what have you got against Wynn?"

"I'm prejudiced."

"The war's been over a long time. Forget it," I said.

"I go by our Monument of Honor every day and I stop. Those names mean something to me. Billy, Harvey, Dwight, Walter—I knew them. They were my friends. I don't intend to forget it."

"If you'd known the bones are an Asian's, would you have told anyone?"

"I said before, somebody somewhere wants to know what happened."

"Carleton, I can't figure you out."

"Pretty soon you're going to have to," he answered. Then he held up his empty glass. Molly brought him a full one.

"Go over the top of the hill behind the Proctor house," Carleton said. "That was the old trail. Go down the other side. You'll come to a stream. Walk north. Keep your eyes open. You'll see where the state boys made a mess. You might want to wear some bright colors. Hunting season's started."

I phoned Wynn. I lied and said I was busy and couldn't take her to dinner. I offered to bring her something from the market. She wasn't hungry, she said. I wanted to be by myself, but I ended up at Jimmy's. Jimmy and the deputy own a boat together. Jimmy told me something the deputy told him: There weren't any buttons or bits from a belt or suspenders or shoe leather. The man didn't have on any clothes when he died.

I didn't mention that fact to Wynn the next day. At the stream she walked ahead of me. In a few minutes we found the place: foundation stones, rotted timbers tossed aside, disturbed earth. She stared at the ground for a long time.

Finally she spoke. "You think the husband killed the chauffeur because he discovered their intimacy?"

I nodded.

"Do you think he cared that much?"

"I don't know what he thought," I said.

She put her arm through mine, and we walked back the way we came. That night we dined at The Proctor once more.

"You may ask me," she said.

"All right, what did the earth say?"

"I've already told you," Wynn answered.

"You asked me if the husband cared enough to kill his wife."

"Which is to ask . . ." She paused and waited, looking out the window as if she could see something in the dark.

"Whether someone cared more than he did?"

She turned to me again. "Precisely, Rudy," she said.

We spoke very little after that. She looked at me and I looked at her. "Are you reading my mind?" she asked.

"I'm trying to read my own."

She reached across the table and held my hands. "I can read your thoughts easily," she said. "The answers are yes and yes."

"Yes, you know how the story ends. Yes, you are leaving."

Her wistful smile matched my own. I drove her to the lake. She thanked me and kissed my cheek and opened the door. A limo service would pick her up in the morning and deliver her to the airport. "I only know how part of the story ends," she said.

I watched the Yankees beating up on Oakland and tried not to think about Carleton. I didn't succeed. I remembered his toast at the party when Debbie and I announced our engagement. I was twenty-five. Carleton stood a bit unsteadily and said he would like to be twenty-five again. He was fifty-four. He talked about being eighteen and shipping out to the Pacific. He rambled on about Billy Proctor and how Billy would have enjoyed the party. Carleton talked about Debbie's mother dying when Debbie was a freshman in college, how she was a good girl and had quit school to take care of him, how much he appreciated that and how he hoped she would return to college one day and finish. He said he liked me and thought I would be a good son-in-law. He said things would work for Debbie and me. When Debbie took off and left me, Carleton shook his head and remarked that he was known to be wrong.

The next day I was going to look for Carleton at the Corners, but out my office window I saw him drive into the inn's parking lot. He sat in his Bronco, waiting.

He offered me one of the beers from the bag on the floor. He said, "I'm going to make this easy for you. I hope you do the same for me."

I tried to get comfortable in the seat beside him. "You, Bud, and Billy had a crush on Mrs. Tillson, didn't you?" I asked.

"You would have too," Carleton answered.

"After you came back from the war, you went over there to see her. You saw them together, Mrs. Tillson and her chauffeur."

"You're half right. I went to visit Billy's mother. She wasn't home. I took a walk. They were at the pond lying bedside each other on a blanket in the sunshine. Before the war he always wore a suit when he drove her to town. White in summer. Black in winter. He didn't have on any clothes now. I went back to Billy's house. Mrs. Proctor hadn't come home. The door was open. I went upstairs and sat in Billy's room. He wasn't coming home, ever. He had taken a handkerchief of hers for good luck. But the person with all the luck was that Jap her husband hired to drive her car. We thought he went away after the war started. She had hidden him, did the driving herself, kept him out of sight. Made love to him. Had carnal knowledge of the enemy."

I started to say something. Carleton held up his hand. "Let me finish," he said. "It wasn't anger. It was too deep for that, what I felt. Even hate doesn't cover it. It was disappointment, the bitterest I've ever known. Profound. I was out of my mind really, or possessed by another one, absolutely rational, absolutely focused. Downstairs was a gun cabinet where Billy kept his rifle. I found a revolver and a box of cartridges in the drawer. Mrs. Tillson had gone inside. The man was still lying on the blanket. I told him to put on his shoes, shiny, soft leather ones. I marched him through the woods. She probably never heard the shot. I took the shoes and covered up the body with timbers and rocks. She was waiting for him. Maybe she had prepared something to eat. She would find his clothes. He had vanished. She would grieve. She would know what I felt for Billy. What others felt for all the missing." Carleton took a deep breath. "Now you've heard my confession. It's your turn," he said.

"Am I supposed to absolve you?"

"You're supposed to understand."

"I bet Mrs. Tillson knew what happened right away; it just happened when she thought it wouldn't anymore. The fact is you weren't sure if the man was Japanese, or Chinese, or Korean, or something else. And we don't know now. But Mrs. Tillson thought people would assume he was Japanese and that put him in danger. She was right."

"I want to you to understand *me,* Rudy. *Me.* Not her."

"I understand why you did what you did. I might have done the same thing myself."

"No, Rudy, you wouldn't. You study things too much."

"Now you want to find out if you did what you think you did, if the man you killed was really the enemy or just someone who looked like he was. So you uncovered the bones, and yourself too."

"A crime of passion. A crime of pain. Real passion, real pain. A crime of patriotism. In a trial, Rudy, how would I come out?"

"It's not going to come to that."

"Say it does. Guilty or not guilty?"

"Not guilty."

He smiled. "That's what I think too."

Carleton reached for another beer. I hadn't tasted mine. I handed it to him and opened the door.

"So tell me, that Oriental . . . that Asian gal turned you on?"

"It's easy to do," I said. I slammed the door as hard as I could.

Carleton leaned across the seat and rolled down the window. "What did I say?" he asked.

It was dark now. I saw the bus stopping up the street. I said, "It's what you're thinking, Carleton. She was more than someone to go to bed with."

"Who was she then?"

"Truthfully, I have no idea. But if I could make her anyone I wanted to, I'd choose Mrs. Tillson."

"She's dead."

"That much I know, Carleton."

"You believe in ghosts, Rudy?"

"Of course I do."

Carleton said, "You're a fool, Rudy." But I could barely hear him. I was halfway across the parking lot.

A few weeks later Carleton phoned the office and asked if I was ever going to drink with him again. I drove to the Corners. The TV was off. The Yankees had won the World Series. What else was new?

"She is," Carleton said.

Molly had quit. The woman Dokey hired to take Molly's place was wearing the same jeans and shoes she had on when I drove her to the bus stop. The Western shirt Dokey had given her didn't fit very well.

Dokey knew what I wanted and sent it over. The woman set my Johnny Walker on the table. She looked into my eyes but didn't say anything. For a second our faces were so close together I could smell her breath. Then she turned away.

"You know her or something?" Carleton asked.

I told him I'd seen her around.

"Today's Billy's birthday," Carleton said. "I'm probably the only person in town who remembers." I raised my glass. "To Billy," I said.

"Every year I write our senators to remind them. I finally got a letter back. A wing from a P-54 was found on a mountainside on one of those Pacific islands. That's what Billy flew. The numbers are still there. It wasn't his plane. But it shows you, doesn't it? They find stuff all the time. The next one could be his."

"Could be," I said.

I drove home and thought about Helen Turley. Her mother had been the town clerk going back to the forties and now Helen was. The town archived its records in one of the old college buildings, which had once been a gymnasium and wasn't safe for students to use anymore. The town never threw away anything. Helen didn't object to my looking. She warned me to take a decongestant because of the dust.

I needed several hours to find it, an application for a chauffeur's license filed by a Mr. S. Ito in June 1940. If my mother were alive, she could tell you something about him, but I can't, Helen said. I made a copy of the application and took it to my office. I wanted to send the copy to Wynn but I had no idea how to find her. I drove to the Corners, but no one had seen Carleton. Cheryl was working by herself. The new girl didn't come to work today, she said.

A professor at the college told me *Ito* was a common name in Japan. I phoned Carleton's house and left my information on his answering machine. I was surprised Carleton had an answering machine. I wondered how many people ever called him.

I'd forgotten what day it was. A car full of trick-or-treaters stopped in front of my house. I had enough apples and Hershey Kisses to go around. The sky was dark and a fine snow was falling. What's New Hampshire without a little snow in October?

I left on the porch light. Flakes glistened on the soft black hat she had pulled down to cover her ears. The snow melted as she waited for me to saying something. I asked if she would like a cup of tea.

She held the cup in both hands and brought it to her lips. She put down the cup and lit a cigarette. I asked her why she was here. You have something to give me, she said.

"It's for Wynn," I said.

"I give it to her."

She folded the copy of Mr. Ito's application and slipped it into her pocket. I liked the way her skin smelled. She finished her cigarette and her tea. She put on her coat.

"You can stay if you want," I said.

"Your friend told me the same thing."

"You mean Carleton?"

"He have a no-good heart. Wynn said your heart good."

"Is Wynn your mother?" I asked.

"Of course not," she said.

"Who is she?"

"Mr. Ito's brother's daughter daughter."

"Granddaughter, you mean."

She shrugged.

"Who are you?" I asked.

"I am not important," she said.

She stepped outside. I watched her walk up the road until I couldn't see her anymore.

In the morning Bud Bryson asked if I'd heard about Carleton. Some trick-or-treaters had found his door open. Carleton was in bed. He hadn't been dead very long. Bud hesitated. His fingers tugged at his beard. "Someone may have been in bed with Carleton. Doc thinks he had a heart attack," Bud said.

"Any idea who?" I asked.

"There was a saucer full of cigarette butts on the bed table. The deputy's sending those to the state lab. He's looking for a new girl who worked at the Corners. I think she's going to be hard to find."

"That's what I think too," I said.

By the end of November a new president had been elected, though no one knew who he was, and a foot of snow covered the ground. The Japanese government had requested the bones. The governor had her picture taken shaking hands with the official from Tokyo. The governor used the opportunity to say once again how small the world had become, how we were all neighbors, and how one day we would all get along. A plane with the bones took off and disappeared into a sky bright and clear as glass. I thought if I could get close enough, I could look through it to the other side and see if anyone was looking back.

~ NAKED ~

The end of December was not the easiest time of the year for Arlene to exercise more, but she was trying. She had been snowshoeing for an hour. The last light was thinning from the sky. She was tired. Wind stung her face, numbed her fingers. As she shoed along Pleasant Street, she realized that if she could cut across Judge Prior's property, she would be home in ten minutes instead of twenty.

The judge had a reputation for being fussy, imperious. He had lived alone for several years in an 1830s Colonial that faced the street. Arlene had been inside once. She remembered rooms small and dark, low ceilings, lots of fireplaces. In the windows Arlene could see electric candles on but no other lights. The snow in front of the garage was plowed, but she saw no tire tracks. Like so many Jeffrey residents, the judge had probably gone south for the winter. Arlene decided to take the shortcut.

The ground sloped away from the street. As Arlene angled in the direction of a row of spruces, the snow around her began to sparkle. She turned to see that a room had been added to the back of the house, one she'd never seen before and couldn't see from the street. The walls were glass. Blazing light filled the room and spilled across the snow. She could make out a pool and trees. She came closer. Judge Prior stood on the other side of the glass observing her. He was naked.

Arlene was too astonished to do anything but gape. For a second she thought the judge was fanning himself, then she realized he was gesturing for her to come in. Now he was pointing at her feet. She bent over and released the bindings of her snowshoes. A door slid open and Arlene stepped into the room.

"I'm glad it's you," the judge said. The comment deepened Arlene's amazement. "When you find your tongue, I'm Max. Remember?"

"I'm sorry," Arlene managed to say.

"Don't be sorry. You'd best take off some clothes. You won't be comfortable if you don't. Your coat at least."

Arlene unzipped her parka and laid it neatly on the floor, which she realized was the source of the room's extraordinary warmth. The judge . . . Max . . . kept looking at her, so Arlene pulled her sweater over her head and dropped the sweater on top of her parka.

Max placed his hand on Arlene's shoulder and steered her toward a cart adorned with bottles. Crotons rose from clay pots near the pool. Trees in larger pots spread their branches on the other side of the room.

"Special lights in the ceiling. Everything grows," Max said.

Arlene glanced up. When she looked down, Max was pouring Tanqueray into a silver martini shaker.

"I've always considered you a handsome woman," Max said.

Arlene could do little more than smile and try not to stare at the judge's body.

"One of these and you'll relax." Max removed a chilled glass from the small refrigerator on the floor near the wheels of the cart. He filled the glass and handed it to Arlene.

Arlene let the first sip warm its way down her throat before she said anything. "Max," she asked, "are you all right?"

"I have nothing to hide. You tell me."

"That's not what I mean."

"You mean, am I sane? If so, why am I naked? Am I auditioning for *Lear*? Do I intended you any harm?"

"The first question, anyway."

"I think I'm quite sane. The rest of the house is old and dreary. Evelyn liked historical homes, so we bought it. When she died I should have moved, but I didn't. Instead I added this room. The architect was involved with the biosphere."

"It is warm," Arlene said.

"Take off more."

Arlene considered what the judge could see—her white socks, purple ski pants, a sports pullover guaranteed to wick the sweat away from the skin—and what he couldn't. "I'm not prepared to drink this martini, which is very good, by the way, in my underwear. I'm even less prepared to be naked," she said.

Arlene wandered around the room and sipped her drink. She thought if she were alone she might take off her clothes. She was beginning to feel languid, the tiredness almost gone from her legs. But she wasn't alone. She circled back to the judge.

"I don't spend all my waking hours like this. When it's getting dark outside, I turn up the heat, have a swim, have a drink, have a little supper. You'll notice after a while the light penetrates your skin. You'll feel better. Feel younger. I actually believe I look younger. I certainly think younger. We're about the same age, aren't we?"

Arlene nodded. She had done more than sip her martini. Ten years before, she could drink three and be coherent. Now she was lucky to manage two, slowly.

"You're almost ready for another," Max said.

Beyond the rim of light, the snow disappeared in the darkness: the way home. "I'm fine right now," Arlene said.

When the judge turned his back, Arlene's eyes wandered over his body, which appeared much firmer and stronger than she would have guessed. Especially his hips. He turned around. She quickly focused on his face. A sheen of dampness covered her own. The judge was right. The heat was penetrating.

"What is the temperature?" she asked.

"Eighty air. Ninety pool. The water is filtered through a separate UV process to purify it. That's why there's no chlorine smell. Just a whiff of jasmine tonight, and orange blossoms."

Arlene began walking again, toward the pots of tall trees. She knew the judge was watching her. She remembered a time years before when she had modeled an evening dress in the garden club fashion show, walking along the runway with feline arrogance. She had been forty then and having an affair with Bradley Templeton. She was aware of the judge following her, aware of his breathing, his scent.

"Arlene, you know if you keep wearing all those clothes they'll be damp and you'll chill when you leave."

The notion of leaving was a good one. "I ought to go now," Arlene answered. The glass felt weightless in her hand.

"You don't really want to, do you?"

"Soon," she said and held out her arm. The glass disappeared. The judge had it now.

Arlene followed him to the cart. "You said you considered me handsome. I didn't know you considered me at all," she said.

"Oh yes. Lately more and more. Around town I see you everywhere. You look fifty."

"So do you."

"Looks can be deceiving."

"But not in your case."

"You can't see inside me."

"You're right about that," Arlene said.

"I wish you could, though. I wouldn't disappoint you."

They walked toward the pool this time, toward a wicker settee and low table by the water. "I usually eat my supper sitting here," the judge said.

"Do you cook?"

"My housekeeper prepares something. I heat it up. She leaves at two. I manage by myself on the weekends."

The pool was a sunset pink that made the water appear pink as well. Arlene had never considered water intimate before. She did now. The color was oddly sensual. A quick swim, then she would finish her drink and go home.

"Max, do you have a robe I could borrow? I can't resist the pool."

"Will a towel do?"

"A large one."

While the judge took a towel out of an armoire decorated brightly with painted iris and tulips, Arlene looked around for a place to undress.

"In the house. Choose any room."

A sensible suggestion, but leaving the room to take off her clothes seemed prudish. Yet Arlene wasn't quite ready to pull them off in front of the judge.

"What are you laughing about?" he asked.

"I'm wearing the tattiest underwear I own," Arlene said.

The judge smiled. "I'll stand across the room," he said. "I won't look."

Arlene took off her shirt, then her socks. Her trousers crinkled when she pulled them down. She bundled up her underwear and pushed it into her trouser pocket. The water was as soft as it looked. She stroked toward the other end of the pool, the judge watching her.

I must be drunk, she thought. She had never experienced water this way. It caressed her as she traveled over it. But she knew she wasn't drunk, only peaceful and content. The judge watching didn't make any difference. In fact she liked it. She had liked walking on the runway, flirting with all the men in the room.

Arlene swam two laps. The judge, who stood at the opposite side of the pool, had thoughtfully laid the towel by the ladder. Arlene climbed out and wrapped the towel around her. The towel almost covered her completely. She raked her hair with her fingers. She noticed that he had added more gin to her drink

"I have cigarettes. You'd like one, wouldn't you?"

"How did you know?"

"I know some things about you."

"Then you know I shouldn't."

"I'm not your doctor."

The judge returned with a teak cigarette box.

"Sure you don't mind?"

"I smoke a cigar from time to time."

They walked back to the settee and Arlene's clothes piled by the edge of the pool.

"You're going to be hungry soon."

"Max, this is lovely, but I'm going to finish my martini and make my way home."

"Of course you're not. What a foolish idea."

"Max . . ."

"The housekeeper always prepares too much for one person. Lamb chops tonight. I can't eat more than one. A salad. Potatoes. Scalloped, I think."

"Max . . ."

"I'm going to the kitchen. You can put some clothes on or not, whatever makes you comfortable."

The judge disappeared into the house. Arlene dried herself. Her shirt was long enough to cover her faded Jockey underpants. She was finishing her martini when the judge returned carrying a tray with two dinner plates and a salad bowl. He set the table by the water, then vanished into the house again for salad plates, wineglasses, and a bottle of Pinot Noir. She realized she had become accustomed to his nakedness and was comfortable looking at his body. They sat side by side, his thigh almost touching hers. She had a fuzzy sensation on her skin, what she felt when she turned on the television and the tiny hairs on her arm received a static charge from the screen.

The lamb was pink in the center, the way she liked it. The Pinot was smooth, full of its advertised flavors. Arlene's contentment deepened. It was more than a pleasure about physical things, the meat, the wine, her skin, the scents of orange and jasmine, the color of the water, the shapes of the pots, the light on the leaves: It was spiritual as well. Wasn't this the peace she was supposed to achieve in all those yoga classes she attended, and never did?

"Max, you're amazing," Arlene said.

"I would say the same about you."

"I feel very still and complete right now."

Arlene imagined saying that to Bob Dorsey, a retired stock trader and deal maker she'd been seeing. He would smirk and tell her she was supposed to tell him that later on, after what he referred to as the main event.

"I think everyone's past is full of regrets. But when I'm in this room, I regret nothing. Out here the past doesn't seem to mean much," Max said.

Arlene smiled and pressed her palm against the judge's thigh and didn't consider whether or not she should have done it.

"Do you think about the future?" Arlene asked.

"You mean tomorrow or the future future?"

"The future future."

"I think about what we all think about, dying on our own terms, the way we want to go. I'd like my heart to stop suddenly while I'm in this room. To cease upon the midnight with no pain, as Keats put it. What about you?"

"When I was coming up the street and it was almost dark, I remembered my mother tucking me into bed. I always hid under the covers. I was afraid of the cold."

"Why?"

"It seemed so impersonal, so empty. You could get lost in it and no one would find you. People would forget about you. "

"Sounds like the future future."

Arlene pointed to the two cigarette ends in the ashtray by the wine bottle. "The future future will be here sooner than I think if I don't give up cigarettes."

"I think you ought to give up Bob Dorsey."

"You know a lot about me, don't you?"

"Not all I want to know. Men must have asked. Why haven't you married?"

"Men hide things. You find out what when it's too late."

The judge laughed. "As you can see, I have nothing to hide."

"I'm not so sure. We all do. The truth, I didn't want to settle down with one man."

"Didn't, or don't?"

"It's been awhile since I had to make a choice."

The judge resisted asking anything more complicated than if Arlene would like coffee. "I can make espresso," he offered.

Coffee before walking home might be a good idea. She could dress while the judge was in the kitchen.

"Or a brandy," Max offered.

"Lord, Max, I don't need anything more to drink. I'll never get home."

"What's at home?"

"My bed, for one thing."

"And probably a message on your machine from Bob."

"Probably."

Arlene was trying to decide the coffee question. It would be a shame to ask the judge to go to a dreary kitchen and make coffee.

"I wish you wouldn't leave."

"Max . . ."

"I've had a crush on you. Do people still use that word? Anyway, I've had a crush on you for a long time."

"Max, I have a phone. You could have called."

"This room wasn't ready yet."

"Were you ever going to phone me? Or did you assume I was going to stop by?"

"You're here, aren't you?"

"Max, I took a shortcut. Don't make a big thing out of it."

"If you insist on going home, I'll insist on driving you."

"Max, I'll be dressed and out of here before you can find your clothes and keys."

The judge rose from the settee. He stood behind her, his hands on her shoulders, as if he was pressing down on her to keep her from leaving. He bent over and nuzzled her neck.

"What do you like about me, Max?"

"You're independent. You're strong. You tell people the truth. And you have long legs."

"You sure you're not just lonely and I have a reputation?"

"You're talking about the past. Out here I don't live there anymore," he said.

"You can't stay out here all the time."

"I wish you wouldn't be so logical."

"You mean you wish I wouldn't bring up the truth."

"What's logical isn't always true."

"Max, the truth is that this has been a lovely and completely unexpected evening, and now it's time for me to go home."

"I'm not going to drive you."

"I don't want you to."

Arlene raised herself off the settee. The judge sat down and watched her put on her clothes.

"Please excuse the cliché, but it's not having regrets that matters, it's having nothing to regret."

Arlene, about to slide open the door, peered into the night. She turned round.

"Change your mind?"

"Yes," she said.

She knelt by the settee and looked up a him. He bent to kiss her. She pressed her finger to his lips.

"Max, phone me. I mean it," she said. A minute later she was on her way home. Having nothing to regret had never been her problem.

She was sorry, though, when Max didn't call. Lois Carey called, and so did Bob. Lois explained she had gone to her doctor for a checkup, and now, three days later, she was phoning from the hospital to report that the surgeon had taken all her breast but the cancer hadn't spread. She would be going home in a few days, and her daughter was coming from Louisville to be with her.

Arlene remembered a New Year's Eve twenty years earlier when Lois was furious with Forrest, her husband, and the two women had stood on the porch of someone's house drinking and smoking. Through the window they could see Forrest dancing with Vera Deemer, who was wearing something red and tight and very low cut. Lois was trying not to cry. "At least you're discreet," Lois said. "Forrest never is," she said. She held out her arms in a gesture of surrender or helplessness. They could hear the music from the phonograph. Arlene put down her own glass and Lois's next to it. Arlene fitted herself against Lois, and the two of them danced, a bit awkwardly at first, Lois's moist cheek pressed to Arlene's. They danced beyond the end of the record, and past another also, their bodies close together, Lois's arm around Arlene's neck. "I can't believe how nice this is," Lois said. Then she stopped dancing and stood for a moment in Arlene's arms and placed her hands on Arlene's face as if she were going to whisper something, but instead kissed her. "I'm better now," Lois said, "let's go inside."

Bob's message was cheerier. Arlene had told him she was going by herself to a party at the Knolls, a community of one-floor condos and apartments popular with people in their eighties and referred to as God's waiting room. Arlene would probably be the youngest person there. She would end up helping guests find their coats and walking several widowers to the elevators or assisting them across the frozen courtyard. The widows usually managed to get home by themselves. Sometimes the men would try to kiss her. One or two always produced a sprig of mistletoe from an overcoat pocket and waved it over her head, as if performing a magic act. But she was the one with the act. She left a trace of lipstick on their cheeks, something to discover when they looked at themselves in the mirror, something to smile about and make them feel they weren't so old after all.

Bob explained that his brother and his sister-in-law had planned to spend the evening at Bob's house, but they had canceled to stay home and fight off the flu. "Let's drive to Boston," Bob said, "and stay at the Ritz."

Decorations glittered in the lobby. Arlene loved hotels. She loved the Ritz. A man in a pressed uniform followed them into the elevator with their luggage. Bob tipped him generously. Bob wanted to shower before going down to the bar for cocktails. Arlene tried to nap, but questions kept her awake. Could she infer from Bob's explanation that had his brother felt better, Bob wouldn't have phoned? She was okay for the Ritz but not okay for family? And why was that? Then there was the big question, the one she always asked herself in the year's last gloaming: Are people responsible for how they end up?

Bob emerged from the steaming bathroom, a towel around his waist. Treadmills and racquetball kept him slender. He was five years younger than she. Was it the age difference that Bob didn't want to explain to his brother and his sister-in-law? And would she really want to meet Bob's sister-in-law? Bob had been divorced for ages. Arlene didn't need an evening with a woman who could compare her with other women in Bob's life, someone who might even take Arlene aside and give her a list of her offenses as evidence that Arlene wasn't in Bob's league. Arlene had her own list.

While Bob shaved, Arlene unzipped her overnight bag. Bob was particular about what pleased him. He preferred her to wear stockings, and underwear in shades of brown. La Perla was his favorite. Because stockings felt more comfortable than panty hose, Arlene often wore them for herself. The male fetish for them amused her, but it irritated her when men told her how to dress. This evening, though, Arlene was willing to oblige Bob. She let him watch her dress, though standing in front of the TV set flipping the channels, he pretended not to. She clipped the tops of her stockings to her garters and drew her palm along the backs of her legs the way she had learned from her mother to be sure her seams were straight. These stockings didn't have seams, but the gesture was part of the performance. Once her mother had turned to Arlene and said, "I wonder what kind of man you'll end up with." Arlene had replied, "Why do I have to end up with one? Or any?" "Child, don't be foolish," her mother had chided her.

In the bar Bob chose a table near the windows. Lit by Christmas lights, the trees in the Public Gardens appeared artificial, like props in an allegory. She was glad to be inside with Bob listening to the piano player and drinking a splendid cocktail. For a second the judge came into her mind, then Bob leaned closer and caressed her hand. "You'll hear about it next week, but I want to tell you now. I'm buying the Jeffrey Trust. That is, a group I put together is buying it."

Arlene wondered if Bob really wanted to run the town's small bank or couldn't resist deal making. You know who you are when you make a deal, he had told her. Or who you are not, she thought, but said nothing, only smiled as if impressed by his insightfulness.

"Congratulations," she, tinging the rim of her glass against his.

"There's a rumor you have a buyer for the Weir farm," Bob said.

"I've heard that myself."

"Not going to tell?"

"I have a prospect, but the farm's been on the market for two years and I've had prospects before."

"The Weir who owns the convenience store next to the bank, what relation is he to the family selling the farm?"

"Buck's a cousin," Arlene said.

"Does he profit when the farm sells?"

Arlene shook her head. "He lives in a room over the store. It's about all he has. Why are you asking?"

"We'd like his property."

"I'm sure he's not interested in selling."

"We know he isn't," Bob said.

"Is there a problem?"

"Not for us, for him maybe. He's going to have to stop selling gas or replace his tanks. That's expensive."

"A lot of people buy gas there."

"I know. I also know he'll come to us for a loan to replace the tanks."

"Then what?"

"We'll lend him the money. That's what a community bank does. We support the community. That's not going to change just because some new guys are running it."

The piano player was playing "Stardust." Bob hummed to himself. Arlene remembered lying in bed after making love with a man waiting to be shipped overseas. She was pregnant then and hadn't told him. If he had come back, if he had married her, would they have stayed in love, stayed together? Or was that question answered by the question Arlene had asked her mother, why only one? Bob ordered another round of drinks. After a few sips the questions slipped out of mind.

The champagne and dinner Bob ordered in the main dining room were extravagant. He winked at her and

[144]

said, "Deal making excites all my appetites. I'm glad you're here."

And Arlene was glad also, except from time to time she wondered what the judge was doing, wondered if he was sitting by himself, feeling young and feeling no regrets. New Year's Eves were always full of regrets as far as Arlene was concerned. She excused herself. "Don't be long," Bob said.

Two ladies sat in front of the mirror. Both wore shimmering evening dresses. In their handbags, open on the marble counter, Arlene noticed the matching gold cigarette cases. Arlene wanted a cigarette. Bob hated the smell of smoke. Arlene walked behind the ladies into the next room. The attendant said, Good evening. When Arlene finished, the attendant handed her a towel and wished her a happy New Year. Arlene placed a folded bill on the tray near the soaps.

The ladies were still sitting in front of the mirror. One was leaning forward, penciling her eyebrows. The other held a lit cigarette between the tips of her fingers. The one looking in the mirror smiled and turned around. "You want a smoke, don't you?" she said. Her voice was amused, ironic, surprisingly rough but not unkind.

"Not allowed," Arlene said.

"Says who?" the one smoking asked.

"My date," Arlene said.

The lady held out her hand. "One drag, he'll never know."

Arlene hesitated, then lifted the cigarette from the fingers and brought it to her mouth and tasted the other woman's lipstick and remembered kissing Lois. Arlene inhaled and gave back the cigarette. She felt a bit dizzy, as if the room had taken a spin and the door wasn't where she expected it to be. She breathed deeply, thanked the woman, and returned to the table.

Bob wasn't there. He had probably gone to the men's room. Arlene looked at the empty chair and imagined Vi, her daughter, sitting in it. But Vi didn't know she was Arlene's daughter. Arlene had tried to tell her. Once in the taproom at the inn she had almost told her. But she didn't. The room turned all blurry. She wiped her eyes before Vi noticed anything was wrong. She was wiping them again right now.

"You okay?" Bob asked.

Arlene looked up. "Fine," she said. "I'm fine."

After coffee, they went downstairs and danced and drank more champagne. At midnight Bob kissed her. Later, in their room, Bob undressed her and they made love. He fell asleep. She slipped out of bed meaning to find her nightgown. She walked to the window. Bob had left on a small light. Arlene could see her reflection. She bent forward until she couldn't see herself anymore. She closed her eyes and leaned her forehead against the glass. She had the sensation of passing through herself and being suspended in the air above the street. She hovered there filling her lungs with darkness. She opened her eyes. A man stood in the window on the other side of the street. He was gesturing with his hands, like the judge, except she was naked this time. She stepped back from the window. The man shrugged and blew her a kiss.

"How was Boston?" the judge asked.

"You mean how was my New Year's Eve in Boston with Bob? Good. What did you do?"

"Thought about you."

"I have a phone."

"That's not romantic."

"But my passing by unplanned is?"

"You're here again, aren't you? Are you comfortable?"

Arlene had come prepared this time. She was wearing silk trousers and a thin blouse. "I'm fine, Max. And this visit isn't unplanned."

"Yes, that unplanned stuff works only once."

"Max, I realize you know everything, so you're aware that Bob heads a group taking over the Jeffrey Trust."

"I am."

"Bob's interested in Buck Weir's property next door."

"Why?"

"He didn't say."

"He probably wants to use the building to expand the bank's trust facilities."

"My concern is Buck. He has to replace his tanks or stop selling gas. The bank will lend him the money.

He'll need fifteen, maybe twenty thousand. The bank already holds a note on the property. Buck trusted the old group at the bank to take care of him and give him good advice. He'll think the new people are like the others. He won't be able to pay off all that debt. He'll lose his property."

"Anything else on your mind?" Max asked.

"I'd like a martini," Arlene said.

Arlene's eyes studied the judge's body as he walked across the room. Why was she still attracted to men, why were they attracted to her? Did she cause that? Did she make that happen? Would she want it to be any different? A definite no to the last question.

The judge handed her a chilled glass. He had brought the cigarettes too. She took a sip. "Do you feel it?" he asked.

"It burns a little."

"Not the gin, the room. Arlene, you look so young. Do you feel young?"

She took another sip and lit a cigarette. "Truth, Max, no. I don't feel young. If anything, I feel a bit awkward, a bit overwhelmed, and very lucky. My mother died when she was sixty, but I've made it this far. I'm still functioning, life is still full of surprises and pleasures, more than I deserve. I have definitely not lived a life of virtue."

"But you're here because you want to help someone. You're worried about Buck."

"If I had the money, I'd lend it to him myself, not charge him interest."

"I do have the money. I can help."

"Can or will?"

"You mean, are we bargaining?"

"Are we?"

"Arlene, come live with me and be my love."

"Is that an answer?'

'It's what's called a proposition or a proposal, depending on your point of view."

"Max, has anyone else discovered this room?"

"Only you."

"You shouldn't waste it."

"I hope I'm not. If I lend Buck money, Bob's going to hear about it. He may not want to see you anymore."

"So helping Buck makes you think you'll have me all to yourself?"

"Arlene, you have a way of viewing a good deed with suspicion."

"Amusement, not suspicion."

"Are men more amusing than women?"

"Absolutely."

"Are women more honest than men?"

"In my experience."

"Are women betters lovers?"

"I have no experience in that regard."

"I saw you kissing Lois Carey once."

"That happened."

"Just once?"

"Once with Lois."

"With anyone else?"

"Max, this isn't court and you're too old to ask dumb questions."

"I've always enjoyed knowing the stuff lawyers couldn't tell the jury."

"In my case there's more rumor than truth."

"You're not going to sleep with me tonight, are you?"

"As foreplay, this conversation hasn't done much for me, Max."

"This room doesn't make you feel what I feel, does it?"

"Max, I feel afraid here. If I stayed in this room too long, I think I'd become unglued. I'd lose my grip on things. If I could live my life at the Ritz, I wouldn't do that either."

"Then what do we do?"

"I put on my boots and coat and go home. One evening I'll be back. I'll surprise you."

"Come when it's very cold outside. It will be very warm in here. It's always warm in here. It's always cold outside."

Arlene gave the judge a quick kiss and then was out the door. The winter constellations glimmered in the sky. Her boots crunched over the snow. Cold enfolded her. She wouldn't have it any other way.

∽ THE APOLOGIST ∽

Hoyt stood on Main Street shading his eyes while he peered at the display of his newest poems in the bookstore window. He had forgotten how low the sun was at four o'clock in February in New Hampshire, but he had not forgotten how cold the evening coming on could be, a clear, starry evening, the moon full and shining on the mountains. His face on the book jacket struck him as youthful, although he knew it wasn't.

His reading was scheduled for eight in the town library, a post-and-beam structure that had once been a barn where fugitive slaves slept in the straw. How many citizens would forsake their fireplaces to hear him? Not many, he thought. Nor would many students give up the basketball game at the college to sit under the dark portraits to listen to words that required concentration and a wider frame of reference than most of them possessed. A few people he'd gone to school with might show up, and a couple of unpublished writers as well would be there to prove to themselves that their work was better than his. Perhaps a young woman would sit where Hoyt could watch her reactions, a young woman listening carefully, stroking her soft hair, knowing he was attracted to her and was addressing each poem to her with his eyes. Wish on, he told himself.

The store smelled of paper and furniture polish. The grain of the shelves glowed in the light, a good light to read in. The two ladies standing in the middle of the store in the rectangle of counters and computer screens and greeting cards welcomed him. He thanked them for ordering extra copies of his book and signed the copies spread on the counter. A few times he had lingered in bookstores in towns where he was reading and watched people open a signed book, turn a few pages, and, more often than not, push the book aside. Once, though, a thin woman, a girl really, had shyly approached him and said his poems made her cry. He had been tempted to say, They're that bad, huh? But she appeared very serious and his humor would insult her. He had bought her coffee at a Starbuck's. She couldn't remember the titles of the poems that made her cry. She attended community college and wanted to be a designer. She had talked about synthetics and ways of cutting fabric. She looked down at the table when she talked, as if she shouldn't talk about herself. They had walked by a river for a while. He had put his arm around her. She wore an old leather coat and he could feel her bones under it. He offered to sign her book. She had lent it to a friend, she said. He didn't believe her, didn't believe she'd read anything he'd written. She had merely matched his face with his picture. You're the first celebrity I've been with, she said. He had felt flattered and angry at the same time.

Hoyt thanked the ladies again, buttoned his coat, and walked up the street to his room at the inn. His room reminded him of the place he and the girl had gone to. A bed, a table, a phone, a chair. Not much else.

Hoyt skimmed the phone book for familiar names. Two of his classmates had their pictures under their ads in the sparse section of the Yellow Pages. One sold real estate. The other operated a cross-country moving business, special Florida rates available. Follow us home, the ad said. Hoyt had taught in schools in Massachusetts, New Jersey, and North Carolina. Maybe Florida would be next.

The couple seated close to the fireplace in the dining room wished him good evening as he passed their table. He chose a seat by the window and ordered a glass of red wine. The bus from Boston to White River Junction let off a passenger at the café. A woman. A man got out of a car and hugged her. Hoyt imagined the cold air on their faces and the warmth under their bulky clothes. That was one of the wonderful things about America—people were always getting off buses or planes, always going somewhere, always leaving here for somewhere else. Hoyt loved to listen to their stories.

Hoyt drank another glass of wine with dinner, then went upstairs to retrieve a folder of poems from his room.

Anne Haber, who had invited Hoyt to read, was waiting inside the library. They hadn't met before.

Anne offered Hoyt a cup of punch from the refreshment table. Hoyt accepted a coffee instead. To put the lie to the notion that you can't go home again, would you accept our invitation to read in your hometown? Anne's letter had asked. Hoyt had moved to Jeffrey when he was fourteen. Except for weekends and summers, Hoyt's father stayed in Boston to be close to his business. Hoyt and his mother had the large house on Brady Lane to themselves. The house was almost empty, most of the furniture in storage. After her divorce, Hoyt's mother returned to Kansas, where she'd grown up. Hoyt didn't think he really had a hometown.

The dour face of James Tuttle, on whose farm the barn originally stood, gazed down from the wall. Hoyt had heard that James Tuttle was not a dour man at all, but instead loved music, cider, venison, and the woman who bore him ten children.

People were arriving. One wanted to return a book and was surprised to discover the library conveniently open so late. He tipped his hat and scurried away. By the time the reading began, Hoyt recognized three or four faces in the audience. He counted thirty people in all. Three percent of the town's winter population. Not bad, Hoyt decided.

Hoyt read a dozen poems, mixing long ones with shorter works, explaining how and when they came to be written. The audience laughed at his humor and enjoyed the local references. They leaned forward to follow one poem in particular, about a man named McCoullough. One winter Mr. McCoullough pulled his house across the frozen lake, a whole day's work for him and his horses and helpers, only to let the house sit on the ice overnight. The wind turned south. In the morning so much fog covered the lake that McCoullough couldn't see to work. The ice softened. The house sank.

At the end of the reading the audience applauded enthusiastically. Hoyt answered a few questions and offered to sign anyone's book, mentioning for those who wished to buy one that the bookstore had several copies.

Only one person approached him. She was about his age, her hair mostly gray. She wore boots, jeans, a wide belt, and a black jacket over a white blouse with a ruffled collar.

"How do you want the book signed?" Hoyt asked.

"I have a pen," she answered.

"No. I mean, do you want me to sign it to you?"

She blinked and shook her head. Her dark eyes looked at him. There was something in their expression he remembered.

"Just sign your name under where it's printed," she said. He did and returned the book to her.

"I appreciate your buying it," he added.

"I know you do," she said.

The library emptied. Hoyt asked his host if she knew who the woman was. "I've seen her around, but I don't know her name," Anne answered.

Hoyt returned to the inn. He remembered the name. Donna. Donna Fitz. Years ago she had been thin and blond, with a reputation for being easy. Her father owned the bowling alley when there was one. They'd lived near Drake's Pond. Hoyt stole some beers and shared them with Donna one summer night while the owls *whoo*ed in the trees and the moon, a fragile crescent, lay poised over the water. Hoyt had touched her all over, but nothing else. She'd stood up and walked home. I'm sorry, he'd called after her.

Hoyt opened the phone book. Surely she wasn't Fitz anymore. But there she was, D. Fitz, Drake's Pond Road.

Ten o'clock. Too late to call. He could do that in the morning before he left. But he wasn't sleepy. He decided to drive out there. Maybe if he saw a light . . .

The plows had pushed the snow into tall piles. The road narrowed to one lane. He remembered the hill going up to her house and didn't think the traction of his rented Taurus would make it. He stopped, Fitz the name on the mailbox. He saw a light in the front window. He parked in the driveway. His feet crunched across the glaze. He didn't see a bell, so he rapped on the door. A dog barked. The light over the door switched on. The door opened.

Donna was still in jeans. She wore wool socks now and a sweater, its cable stitching unraveling. The air around her smelled of wood smoke and cigarettes.

He said, "It's late but I wanted to apologize. I remembered your name as soon as you left."

Donna calmed the dog. The TV was on. A cigarette burned in the ashtray beside a bottle of Sam Adams.

"I didn't expect you to remember. It's been thirty years. I wouldn't have recognized you either."

"Thanks for coming to the reading."

"No problem. You want a beer?"

"I don't want to keep you up."

"You're not," she said. He patted the dog until Donna handed him a cold bottle.

"You want a glass?"

Hoyt shook his head.

"Sit down," she said. She clicked off the TV.

"I didn't expect to find you here."

"I divorced and moved back after my father died."

"I sorry," Hoyt said.

"Don't be. Dad had throat cancer and wanted to go. My husband wanted to go too."

"Kids?"

"Two boys. One helps me clean cottages and runs errands for my seniors. The other one lives in Colorado and has kids of his own. You?"

"No wife, no kids."

The dog had settled near the woodstove in the corner of the room. Donna sat on the sofa. Hoyt stood between the sofa and the dog. In one of the photographs on the wall he recognized Mr. Fitz holding a rife and kneeling beside a dead bear.

"What you could apologize for is your poem about McCoullough," Donna said.

"Why?" Hoyt asked.

"After he got his house on skidders and his horses pulled it acrost the ice, you say the reason he didn't finish up was he was so prideful of his ability to tell the weather that he didn't see any harm in waiting until the next day."

"That's the story I heard," Hoyt said.

"You heard wrong. The only way pride entered things was his was hurt. The bank sold his land and would have taken his house unless he moved it. He couldn't support his family. He couldn't pay the men helping him. Didn't even have whiskey to offer. He was too ashamed to ask them to stay any longer."

"I apologize again," Hoyt said.

Donna pressed her lips together, nodded, and took a long drink of beer.

"Why don't you sit down?" she said.

Hoyt lifted a pile of newspapers off the chair by the desk. Dreaming, the dog made a sound between a growl and a whine. Its legs trembled. Its claws ticked on the floor.

"Anything else I should apologize for?"

"You probably don't remember . . . no, you probably do, that time at the pond."

"Of course I remember."

"You turned me down. I was poor and you weren't. Poor girls always want something."

Hoyt shook his head. "Money had nothing to do with it."

"Really?"

"Really."

"Are you hungry or anything?" Donna asked.

"I'm fine."

"McCoullough was my great-grandfather," Donna said. "I knew you'd read that poem."

"Is that why you came?"

"I was curious to see how you turned out." She stood up. "I'm hungry. I'm going to nuke some popcorn."

Hoyt followed her into the kitchen. When she stretched for a bowl on the shelf, he glimpsed her skin through the unraveling wool. His desire surprised him.

"Your family has been here a long time, hasn't it?" Hoyt asked.

"Since 1800."

The pops in the microwave subsided. Hoyt finished his beer. Donna opened another and handed it to him. They looked into each other's eyes a second before she took out the popcorn and slit the foil. They leaned against the counter and ate from the bowl between them.

"You're very tidy," she said.

"The way I eat popcorn?"

"The way you pick words. I was impressed."

They looked at each other again. He set down his beer softly and deliberately, taking his time, trying to talk himself out of what he wanted to do, trying to explain to himself why he wanted to do it at all, wishing she would say stop or don't so he could apologize again and leave. She didn't move. He kissed her. Soft, salty lips. She didn't kiss back but she didn't pull away either. He took a breath and kissed her again, his eyes open, hers looking into his. They laughed. She touched his cheek.

"You kiss good," she said.

Then Hoyt leaned down, lifted the hem of her sweater, and kissed her there. She trembled. Her skin was warm and smooth.

"You want to stay over?" she asked.

The bed was narrow. He could feel the cold on the other side of the window behind the curtain. He slid between the chilly sheets. He breathed the smell of her hair on the pillow, familiar and unfamiliar at the same time.

She turned off the light when she came out of the bathroom. She waited until she was in bed beside him before she took off her robe.

"You don't want to see me naked," she said.

Hoyt kissed her some more, her mouth, her breasts. He couldn't tell if she liked him kissing her breasts or not. She had strong hands and massaged his shoulders while he kissed her.

He knelt between her legs. She closed her eyes. He kept his open. Lines spread across her face. She was concentrating on her own journey, where her body was going. She breathed through her mouth, long sighing breaths. Then she said, "Oh," as if a little surprised she'd gotten where she wanted to go.

Hoyt lay with his arms around her. The dog stretched out by the bed and started dreaming again.

All the women Hoyt had slept with were thin and young, like the girl in the bookstore. She had sat on the bed and drawn her legs to her chest. She didn't have much to tell him. She admitted she'd never read anything he wrote and was only practicing. Someday she might get lucky and connect with a rock star, or someone important. Then she had put on her clothes and left. The others stayed longer, some for months, one for a year. They told Hoyt everything they remembered. Then they packed up and moved out, or he did.

Donna wasn't young. She wasn't thin. Donna had stories, her life, the town's life, more stories than anyone else. He would hear them all. She didn't know how rich she was.

Hoyt closed his eyes and listened to the wind blowing. When he left her, in some wintry future, maybe snow would be falling, covering his tracks. Whither he was going, nothing would manifest. The clean getaway he had always longed for.

~ THE MAN WHO KISSED ~ ZASU PITTS

When I was growing up in Jeffrey, every Sunday night my mother and I watched *What's My Line?* I often imagined myself as a guest on the program, signing my name, Whitney Beck, on the chalkboard for the audience to read, then crossing the set and sitting down next to Mr. Daley, the host. The panelists wore blindfolds because I was a celebrity. I would whisper to Mr. Daley my line. My words would appear on the TV screen in case someone didn't know who I was or what I did. What did I do? Sometimes I was a bobsled champion, sometimes a ski jumper, sometimes a speed skater. Growing up in northern New England, one sees one's accomplishments in terms of winter.

I became a copyright lawyer in New York. Neither my name nor my profession was unusual or interesting. Had the program still been on, I would not have been invited. Now that I have returned to Jeffrey, however, my name confers a certain standing, has cachet. I replay the scene. I whisper to Mr. Daley, "My name is Whitney Beck and I'm eligible."

I never met Mr. Daley. I suppose he is no longer meetable. I did make the acquaintance of the celebrities on the panel. Mr. Cerf, the publisher, employed me once in a case involving a claim against one of his authors. Mr. Gabel, the actor with such a marvelous voice, I encountered in the office of my partner. Mr. Gabel was married to Arlene Francis, also a panelist. She was there too. At one of my Harvard reunions I had a drink with their son Peter at the Hasty Pudding Club.

Miss Kilgallen, Dorothy, the fourth member, I came to know better than anyone else on the panel, though we never officially met. My mother was an avid reader of her column. My mother eagerly awaited everything Dorothy wrote about the Sheppard murder trial out in Ohio. Her photograph appeared next to her byline. Neither in print nor on camera was she attractive. Even my mother said so. But I was drawn to her. My fantasy life was very rich and complicated then. I was about twelve. I imagined Dorothy lying in bed with me. She was worldly. When she finished, I was worldly too. My mother wondered how I could use up the box of tissues by my bedside so quickly. My mother has been dead for several years. We often have little chats, though. We're much franker about things than we were when she was alive. I'll have to remind her about the tissues. She may have understood all the time and simply been playing the naive-mother role to save me embarrassment. I was ten when I met ZaSu Pitts.

I'm sixty-three. I'm in my third period of eligibility. I eat out a lot. During my first eligibility, I didn't have time for dating and courting. I focused on my career.

I'm not ashamed to admit I paid for comfort. Quite pricey ladies, well dressed, well spoken, and attractive, would visit me on a weekend night at the hotel of my choosing. Monday morning I was clear-headed, free of commitments, and ready for work. After my career became established, I began a time of escorting disappointed women to parties, to the theater, to bed. They were women whose first marriages had failed. They had gripes about bank accounts, attorney's fees, and school bills, the everyday stuff their therapists weren't interested in. I listened, gave advice, and understood when to stay and when to go home.

Tonight I'm Cal's guest. Cal runs the trust department of a Boston bank. He owns a home in the Back Bay and one here on the lake. We were friends in high school. We play tennis together. Cal's sister, Sylvia, is visiting from Connecticut, along with his niece, who graduated from Dartmouth last month. Cal's a dozen years older than Sylvia. He refers to her as their parents' love child. I didn't know her growing up. She lost her husband a year ago. She's the reason Cal asked me along.

A fine July evening. At the club, I park beside Cal's Lexus. His banker's car, he calls it. His summer car, his MG, is out of storage, but its brakes need work. I notice the green Subaru next to the Lexus, the ski rack on the roof, the Dartmouth stickers on the dusty window, the cargo area filled with cartons of books and clothes, cassettes scattered over the passenger seat.

Brightness lingers in the air. It's hard to think the days are getting shorter again. Light shines on the golden tube of lipstick tucked against the window. The first time I ever tasted lipstick on a woman's mouth was here, in the barroom, when ZaSu kissed me.

In those days the barroom was decorated with golf trophies, snowshoes, and heads of beasts shot in Africa or South America. Soft fabrics and banquettes have replaced the hard chairs and tables. Watercolors of our mountains and lakes adorn the walls. I walk through the room to the side porch. Cal waves at me. There's a martini glass at his place. Sylvia has a white wine. Her daughter, a glass of red. The club serves a good Pinot.

Cal stands and shakes my hand. "You remember Whit," he says. Sylvia smiles. I'm introduced to Torrey. She smiles too. Is it a trick of the light, or do her eyes have the internal sparkle of a fine cognac? She's wearing a black halter dress that compliments her tan. "Two weeks in Florida," she says, understanding my question. Most of us are still winter pale.

"I really don't," Sylvia says, reminding Cal I'm his age, not hers. I sit between Sylvia and Torrey.

Cal says, "Age doesn't make much difference anymore." He glances at Sylvia, then at me.

Sylvia is wearing a linen dress. A matching orange jacket is draped across the back of her chair. The scoop neck of the dress shows off the gold links of her necklace.

Karen appears to take my order. I ask for a Gibson. For some reason I think I sound like an old man ordering an old man's drink. Cal is ready for another martini.

Cal explains to Torrey that my family has been in Jeffrey since the Revolution. A Beck built the first meetinghouse in town.

"A long male line," I add, looking at Sylvia. I'm sure Torrey is put off by the history stuff.

"Do you have children?" Sylvia asks.

"No," I answer. She's thinking the line ends with me. She's too polite to say so. I tell her my half brother has two sons.

Sylvia's eyes work me over, trying to figure out the family dynamics. Maybe a clean family record is a requirement. Obviously she's interested in dating again. I wonder if dating is the right word for what people our age do. I sip my Gibson. Sylvia turns and watches a late foursome putting in the distance. The light is fading from the sky. Torrey's neck is fabulously delicate.

Torrey catches me staring. Her eyes are darker now. She doesn't appear to mind my attention. I open my mouth to inquire about her plans, but Cal needs to give his sister more information. "Whit's never been married," he says.

Sylvia's eyes are probing me again. Torrey's eyes are kinder. "Never met the right woman?" Sylvia asks.

"Something like that," I answer.

"Or the right man?" Torrey asks, without irony.

Cal's eyebrows rise in amusement. "Whit had a bit of a reputation."

"For what?" Torrey asks.

"Torrey, dear, don't be rude," Sylvia remarks.

Torrey leans toward me and touches my hand. "I didn't mean to be rude," she says. Her hand lingers on mine.

"For work," I tell her.

"That too," Cal says.

Someone has told a story and people in the barroom are laughing. When ZaSu came into the room, the laughter stopped. She stood there and let everyone look at her.

"Cal tells me you've retired and moved back to Jeffrey," Sylvia says. "What keeps you busy?"

"I'm learning to be something useful, a grease monkey. An antique grease monkey."

Sylvia doesn't know what to say. She looks at Torrey. Torrey looks at me. "What's a grease monkey?" Torrey asks.

"Denotation or connotation?"

Torrey's frown deepens.

"Both, I guess."

"In the old days gas stations had grease pits. A man could stand up under a car to drain the oil and grease what needed greasing. His hands and face got pretty dirty. He was referred to as a grease monkey. There's also a racial thing you can read into it."

"Whit likes to tinker with cars," Cal says.

"I tinker. The man who works for me is serious. We restore old cars."

"Is there any money in that?" Sylvia asks.

She fingers the links of her necklace. Is she telling me she's expensive?

Not much, I tell her.

Karen informs us our table's ready. Cal and I escort the ladies into the dining room. Torrey's hand brushes mine. She looks into my eyes. There's a pale imperfection in one of hers, a fleck of white in the brown iris. For a second she stands still. I feel her breath on my face.

"An accident in chemistry class," she explains. "I can see fine."

Karen hands us menus. Cal switches to wine. I order another Gibson. Sylvia takes notice. Cal recommends the lobster bisque and the crab cakes. Sylvia asks about the venison. It's from New Zealand, Cal answers. Our drinks come and Sylvia orders the bisque and venison. Cal always chooses crab cakes and a filet. Karen has already penciled them on her pad. I'm the predictable salad and halibut. Torrey orders salad and sole.

"Summers are pleasant here, but the winters would get me down," Sylvia remarks.

"Most of the town moves south," Cal says.

"Do you?" Torrey asks.

"I like snow," I answer.

"What do you like about it?"

"It's quiet."

"And cold," Sylvia adds, as if there is nothing more to say on the subject.

I glance at Cal. From his smile I get the idea he knew Sylvia and I wouldn't hit it off. We're here to amuse him. Karen arrives with our first course. I'm tempted by another Gibson, but I order a Chardonnay.

"Where do you go from here?" I ask Torrey.

"I'm spending the night with a friend from school."

That explains the separate cars, but it's not what I meant.

"Torrey is a filmmaker," Cal says.

"Not quite. Not yet, anyway. I'm a filmmaker wannabe. I start a graduate program at NYU in the fall."

I can't interpret the smile Sylvia beams in Torrey's direction. Maybe she's a proud mother and thinks Torrey will succeed. Maybe she's thinking she'll settle for a wonderful life in Connecticut, the kids, the house, the husband who commutes to the city.

"Do you like movies?" Torrey asks.

"I used to go all the time."

"Any favorite director?"

"Altman, I guess."

"Do you like *Brewster McCloud*?"

"I do."

"We may be the only ones."

"What's it about?" Sylvia inquires.

"Bud Cort is a skinny kid who has fantasies of becoming a bird."

Sylvia thinks that's silly.

"It is and it isn't," I reply.

"Does he get anywhere?"

"He manages to fly inside the Astrodome for a while."

"What happens."

"Gravity," I answer.

Torrey is leaning forward. Her hand squeezes mine under the table. We're allies. Karen is ready to serve the main course.

"Where are you staying tonight?" Sylvia asks.

"With the Glendons," Torrey says. "They're on the lake." She promises to stop by to see her mother and Cal in the morning before driving to Boston.

"Find out if they like their pool," Cal says.

"If you live on the lake, why would you want a pool?"

"It's heated. The lake isn't," Cal replies.

Torrey asks me where I live. I tell her a few houses down the street from the Glendons.

"Since you're into movies," Cal says to Torrey, "do you know who ZaSu Pitts was?"

"I saw *Greed*. She's awesome in it."

"Would you believe," Cal continues, "that ZaSu Pitts once visited here?"

"Really?"

"Would you believe ZaSu Pitts kissed the man you're sitting next to?"

Both Sylvia and Torrey look at me. Torrey asks, "Is that true?"

"I was a kid. It happened a long time ago."

"This venison's quite tender, for venison," Sylvia comments.

Torrey takes a sip of wine. "Was she lost, or what?"

"Dr. Atwell knew her. She was his guest."

"Atwell was the town dentist," Cal explains. "A real character."

I remember the barroom full of smoke and liquor smells and laughter. It stopped when ZaSu came in. Silence, then someone shouted, ZaSu, how 'bout a drink?

Cal says, "When Atwell was seventy, he impregnated his nurse."

Not someone. Felton Cooper did the shouting. Felty. He was bigger than anyone else in the room. People were afraid of him. The gnu's head mounted on the wall, he'd shot it. Once he grabbed me by the seat of my pants and twirled me over his head. My pants tore and people laughed. His wife apologized to my mother.

Sylvia says, "Charming. Was the doctor married?"

"He was a widower by then."

Karen removes my empty glass and puts a full one in its place. More evidence for Sylvia, but I'm not paying attention to her. Torrey is watching me, as if she knows what I'm doing, telling her about ZaSu. ZaSu was taller than I was. But not by much. When she smoked, the smoke seemed to stay where she blew it. I had the feeling the ice didn't melt in her glass. The room quieted down again. She was telling a story. I don't remember what about.

"Whit, did Atwell marry her or not?"

Her? The nurse, he means. "I really don't remember."

"Whit usually remembers everything," Cal says.

I remember people laughing at ZaSu's story. She drank another drink and smoked more cigarettes. I stood on the floor near her legs. She wore a black dress. I could see threads hanging off the hem. The leather on the heels of her shoes was torn. The heels were worn down. She was older than my mother, but I don't know how much. I noticed some of the men talking about her. I knew ZaSu had been famous. My mother told me when you were famous, people dreamed about you. I'll say, my father said. My mother shot him a look. I think I understood what he meant. ZaSu had been in dreams all over the world.

"The town was amazed Doc still had it in him."

Now Sylvia shoots her brother a look. Torrey hides a smile behind her hand.

"Over the years Whit has met a lot of famous people."

"Mostly writers," I explain.

"And how many kisses did you get?" Torrey asks.

"A few polite pecks on the cheek."

"Then ZaSu was a bit more passionate than that?"

"A bit."

"You were a child," Sylvia says.

"That's right. I was."

Sylvia reaches behind for her jacket. Cal and I hold it for her. She wiggles her arms into the sleeves.

ZaSu used some words I'd never heard a woman use before. I could see Felty's bored red face. People weren't listening to him. He'd played football at Cornell. He'd run a railroad. He'd shot animals in Africa. Some of the other men were bored with ZaSu too. Some of the women had heard enough. This heartthrob in broken-down shoes, who did she think she was? She couldn't make it in talkies, could she? Felty yelled, Hey ZaSu, how 'bout kissing the kid? I don't think she knew I was there. She looked down as if she'd lost something. She found me. Everyone in the room wanted to see her kiss me. Her smile was kind, a little sad too. She wanted another drink, she wanted to eat. A kiss wasn't much of a price to pay. I was hoisted up and set on the bar.

"I think I'll skip dessert, but I'd like coffee," Sylvia says.

Karen stands by while the busboy clears the table. We listen to her dessert recitation. Three of us order decaf. Torrey asks for a port. Now it's Cal turn to beam at her. He orders one for himself. I stick with the rest of my wine. I glance at Sylvia for a sign of redemption, however meager. Nothing doing.

"Whit even met all the panelists on *What's My Line?*" Cal comments.

"Except Miss Kilgallen," I remind him.

It takes Sylvia a minute to understand what her brother is talking about. "I don't think that show was on anymore when I came along."

Torrey finishes her port and folds her napkin. She walks around the table and kisses her mother's cheek, then Cal's. I'm ready to leave too.

"Why don't you walk me to my car?" Torrey says.

"I'm sure we'll met again." Sylvia's words lack enthusiasm.

Torrey walks ahead of us. Cal stops at the doorway, squeezes my arm. "Sylvia is being prickly tonight. This meeting men stuff is harder for her than she thought."

I catch up with Torrey. The sky is full of stars. She puts her arm through mine. We walk slowly. Our hips touch. She asks me to finish my story.

"I sat on the bar. ZaSu arranged the scene, brushed my hair away from my eyes, unbuttoned my little wool jacket, placed her palms on my cheeks, moved her hands toward my mouth, leaned her face to mine. I could smell the liquor and cigarettes. The whole room had fallen silent. ZaSu's hands formed a tiny steeple. No one could see if she put her lips on mine."

"Did she?"

"Yes."

"Anything more?"

"Yes."

"You're kidding."

"No."

Torrey stops walking. "Show me."

My fingers tremble a little. They press the warmth of her skin. My lips on hers, barely touching. The tip of my tongue delicate, discreet.

Torrey and I pull apart. "Then what?" she asks.

"People cheered. She had the crowd again."

ZaSu unfolded the handkerchief from my breast pocket and wiped my mouth. She whispered into my ear, Darling, don't listen to anything they say. Then someone put a fresh cocktail in her hand. The room was full of noise. She stood on the edge of it. She seemed to be observing something happening somewhere else, gazing down from her silent screen at the noisy audience amusing itself. She preferred silence. She knew it better than anyone else there.

Torrey clicks the remote in her hand. Her car lights blink on. "Thanks for the kiss," she says. "Too bad you're not someone famous."

"Maybe you'll be," I answer and smile sweetly.

A couple of times that night I thought about her swimming in the pool, or better yet I imagined she phoned and asked me to come over and test the water myself. A voice I recognized as my mother's said, You're not that eligible.

The next morning I was walking my dog. Torrey and her friend were riding toward me on bikes. I wanted to hold up my hand to stop them. I wanted to finish ZaSu's story. Late in her life her career took off again. I didn't, though. Torrey and her friend went by and waved, the way people do up here even to people they've never met.

∽ SOOTY ∽

Sooty Culver was the first person to get one.

I've known Sooty all my life. He was never first at anything. Always a follower. A cautious person, except that time when we were kids. At my sixth birthday party we planned to go swimming in the lake. Sooty's mother forgot his suit. While my mother and Sooty's mother searched for something he could wear, Sooty took off all his clothes and dashed into the water. I and the other boys and girls I had invited were too startled to laugh or make fun of him.

Years later our friend Murray Tate recalled during one of the our blissful New Hampshire summer evenings when we think we're still young enough to indulge in three cocktails that Sooty, at six, appeared more developed in the masculine department than the rest of us. Myra, Murray's wife, said, Don't you guys ever quit this measurement stuff?

Our senior year in high school I was the yearbook editor. I chose the comments that appeared under each senior's photograph. There were only twelve in our class. Under Sooty's picture I wrote, A friend to all. Years later I wouldn't have changed it.

Of those twelve classmates, two stayed in town, four moved away and then returned. Mack and I have never lived anywhere else beside Jeffrey. Sooty, who worked in Boston, and Murray, who worked in New York, moved back. Barbara and Priss returned after their husbands died.

Sooty, Murray, Mack, and I, and our wives, spent a lot of time together. We show our ages, but we're in pretty good health, we think. That's why Marilyn's death shocked us. One afternoon she went home after tennis, mentioned a headache, and told Sooty she was going to lie down. A hour later he couldn't wake her. A stroke, her doctor said.

Mack and I began to study Sooty, what he did, how he coped, how he grieved. We didn't say that's what we were doing, but we did it. We wanted to know how mourning fit him, how it might fit us.

Also we began to speculate on the kind of life Sooty and Marilyn carried on with each other. How intimate were they? How physical had their relationship been, these people, like the rest of us, nourished on Yankee values of measure, decorum, and privacy? A few years earlier, about the time Sooty and Marilyn turned fifty, someone reported seeing them quite passionate in a car at Drake's Pond. Of course, we were thinking about our own marriages, our own intimacies. We winced a bit when Myra asked if we ever stopped measuring ourselves.

Sooty is a retired officer in an accounting firm. He drives to Boston once a month to dine with his former partners and spend the night. He must have bought it then. Priss described it as being the size of a locket, only square, made of dimpled silver. No initials or anything. It hung from his neck on a chain of tiny silver links. Priss told Nancy about it. Nancy told me. I told Murray and Mack.

Nancy and I have been married a long time. She takes after her father. He sold used cars in Claremont and taught her the art of oblique disclosure. We were sipping our evening wine on the patio. Nancy said, I was talking with Priss today and she told me Sooty wears a little silver ashtray around his neck. Nancy asked me if I knew that.

I didn't, nor could I imagine anything but a clunky receptacle for cigarette ends or cigar stubs. Nancy repeated Priss's description of what Snooty was wearing. The silver thing like a locket contained a spoonful of Marilyn's ashes.

I wondered, Had Snooty dug up the urn with Marilyn's ashes that we watched him. kneeling, place in the cemetery ground, or had he kept the spoonful in an envelope in a desk drawer because he had the locket idea in mind already? And how would the idea have come to him in the first place? I refilled my glass and tried to picture it all happening.

Sooty lives on Bishop's Hill. He has a large house and a pool. I asked Nance if Sooty had invited Priss for a swim and that's when she noticed his neckwear. I could see Sooty and Priss reclining side by side on comfortable chaises, sipping drinks, observing Mount

Blue in the distance. She turns to him and notices the silver thing nestled in the white hair of his chest.

Yes and no, Nancy said. Sooty had invited Priss over, but they had been in bed.

"You mean . . . ?"

"That's right."

I really wanted to picture what Nance was thinking. The canvas of my own imagination now filled with the image of Sooty leaning above Priss, the silver thing swaying in the air between them. However, Nance and I are not ones to share our carnal imaginings. I was curious how much Priss had shared with Nancy.

"Are you surprised?" Nancy asked.

"Sooty was always devoted to Marilyn."

"He still is."

"When did Priss find out what was in the silver thing?"

"She didn't interrupt to inquire, let's put it that way."

I saw Priss slipping the chain over Sooty's head and pushing the silver thing under a pillow. Or maybe she turned it around so the silver thing hung down Sooty's back where she couldn't see it. She hadn't asked what it was. It was merely in the way. She asked later, a moment of postcoital curiosity.

"Was Priss surprised?"

I imagined the silver thing was really in the way now. Whose mood wouldn't be disturbed by such knowledge?

"She said she'd forgotten how good sex could make her feel," Nancy answered.

Ambiguity lurked in Nance's response.

"You mean she'd forgotten how sex could make her feel good, or how good sex could make her feel?"

Nance caught the implication of the latter.

"Stop playing lawyer. The sex was good," Nancy said.

I caught the heat of accusation in Nancy's tone.

Alice was the second person to get one.

Ted and Alice Goforth were people we saw at parties in the summers. Alice is Sooty's cousin and an expert gardener. Despite Ted's emphysema, the Goforths went forth to Boca Raton every November and returned to Jeffrey every June. Except this June. Ted died in February. His cremains were interred in South Carolina, where they both had family. Alice didn't appear in Jeffrey until August. She was in good spirits, quite chatty. I believe it was Peg, Mack's wife, who admired the bracelet Alice wore, tiny silver flowers resembling dahlias, the one in the center a bit larger than the others. Alice didn't hesitate to reveal the secret. The larger bloom lifted apart revealing a pinch of Ted's ashes. Peg remarked if she'd sneezed, she'd have blown poor Ted across the room.

Listen, Mack said the next day, there's an investment opportunity here. We need to do some designs, get a line of these things going.

We never followed through. We had the gift of prophecy but not the will to act upon it. Besides, we thought that investing in memory art, the name we gave to jewelry designed to hold the ashes of a loved one, might be bad luck.

However, by November a dozen people we knew or heard about were wearing memory art. At Weed's in Hanover, a jeweler was particularly adept at fashioning the pieces. Gorem Townley, who had been an avid angler, graced his wife's throat inside a golden snook. The dust of Sylvan Bichette, who in life had preferred the company of sports cars to his wife's, filled the shape of a platinum Triumph that jangled on his wife's charm bracelet when she signed checks spending Sylvan's money.

I suppose Peg would put me in a silver golf tee, Mack said. I remarked that a tiny wine bottle would probably be Nancy's choice. We agreed it was a good thing we were both traditionalists who preferred coffins and real burials. *Cremains,* such an awful word. I grimace whenever I hear it.

By this time Sooty had initiated more than one survivor into her carnal twilight. Mack and I were eating lunch at the inn. Outside it was snowing hard for December. We decided to stay in the bar because it was warmer than the dining room. Jimmy had poured us our second round of old-fashioneds. Pretty quiet this time of year, I commented. The skiers are starting to book for the holidays, Jimmy said. We'll be busy. There's the Culver party, too.

Mack and I looked at each other. Sooty's having a party? I asked. Jimmy nodded. Mack and I looked at each other again.

We're not invited, I told Jimmy. Mack asked who was. Jimmy knew only that Sooty had reserved the lounge and some rooms.

Mack and I were finishing our coffee and sampling a port when I suggested what Sooty was up to.

Remember those key parties in the seventies? I asked him. The men dropped their keys into a bowl and went to bed with the women who reached in and picked out theirs.

Mack said, I know what you mean. But I never attended one. You don't think that's what Sooty has in mind, do you?

Not keys, I said. Memory art. I pictured an enormous brandy snifter full of all shapes and sizes.

Would you have gone to one? I asked.

No, but thirty years ago I would have had a few ladies in mind that I would have wanted to choose my key.

Meaning you haven't anyone in mind now?

Do you?

I shook my head. Frankly, the whole idea of any woman besides Nance seeing me naked leaves me cold, I said.

I'm with you, Mack said. When we were young our equipment worked too fast, now it might not work at all. Too much explaining to do.

There always was, I said.

Mack looked into the distance. Do you ever think of Brenda Fraser? he asked.

Brenda Fraser had soft brown hair and pale skin. Every May, just before the blackflies came out, the senior boys dared one another to swim across Drake's Pond. The water was numbing, so cold you could hardly breathe. The week after our swim we heard a rumor that the senior girls were going to do a swim too. Mack and I hid in the woods. There were five girls in the class but only Brenda showed up. She didn't hesitate. She took off her clothes and waded into the water. She swam across the pond, then back again. She emerged from the water and dried herself. I know you're there, she said.

Mack and I waited until she had on clothes again before we stood up. Anything you didn't see? Brenda asked. Mack and I mumbled something. Now it's my turn, she said. Show me what you've got.

Mack and I felt guilty enough to do what she asked. We undid our belts and lowered our pants.

Don't have much, do you? Brenda remarked.

We looked down and examined ourselves. We were pink, and short, and thin as clothesline.

Brenda offered us a deal: Don't talk about me, I won't talk about you. We took it. Mack and I finished our port and left Jimmy a substantial tip.

The next Saturday night I told Nancy I was going to walk to the Stop 'n Go to buy a *Globe*. The store closes at nine. I took the long way home, past the inn. I could hear music and laughter from the lounge. I looked through the window. I recognized Sooty's children. They had children of their own now. The people I didn't know, friends and relatives from out of town, I supposed. There was a birthday cake that hadn't been cut yet. I watched Sooty open his arms to enfold one of his guests.

That's what I had seen so many years ago, Sooty, his arms wide open, running toward the water. Then I realized Mack had it wrong. Sooty wasn't any different on the outside from Mack or me. But on the inside he was different. He was running toward something, his arms open to embrace it. It wasn't just the lake or the rest of us splashing mindlessly in the water. It was something more than that, something comic and sad, something that gave peace and took it away, something we knew nothing about yet.

When I got home, I called out, but Nancy didn't answer. Maybe she had the TV turned up. Or maybe she was tired of waiting and had fallen asleep.

∼ FOG ∼

A Friday afternoon before Memorial Day. Damp breeze. Fragrance of lilacs. White petals strewn across the grass under the apple trees.

The Shippen College commencement had taken place a week before. The town would stay quiet now until Father's Day. The blackflies would stop biting then and the owners of summer cottages on the lake would return, the elderly residents who wintered in Florida or Arizona, crowding Vivaldi's market by nine in the morning, the post office by ten. But now things were slow. You could find a place to park on Main Street. You didn't need a reservation for the dining room at the inn. Only three or four boats appeared on the lake.

Nicki Groh was walking along Main Street in the direction of the bookstore. Wesley Boots stood in front of the bank and watched her, studied her short skirt and brown legs. The Grohs had flown to Honolulu at Easter. Wesley imagined being young again.

Wesley Boots remembered when Sheldon and Harriet had adopted Nicki. She was five. She threw up all the time. She couldn't dress herself. Couldn't talk, only stuttered. At a picnic that first summer, she squatted in front of the guests and peed. Look at her now. Wesley wasn't embarrassed by his imaginings.

Willie Boots, Wesley's son, was Nicki's classmate. In the fall she would enter Princeton. Willie had been turned down at Dartmouth and Penn. He was on the waiting list at Boston University, accepted at Babson.

Anne Haber saw Nicki too. Anne supervised the town library. Harriet volunteered there. She was at home today. Anne had finished reshelving the large-print mysteries. She looked across the street and saw Nicki go into the bookstore. She wondered what kinds of things Nicki read. Nicki was bright, and different, sure of herself. Some other girls called her arrogant and snobby. Those other girls misused *like* all the time and raised their voices at the ends of sentences, turning them into questions. Nicki didn't do those things. She probably didn't read trash, either.

Willie and his friend Mike were driving by when they saw Nicki leaving the store. Willie and Mike were always together. On the baseball team Willie pitched, Mike caught. Hey, man, we're the battery dudes, they would say and slap each other's palm, making the sound of Willie's fastball smacking the pocket of Mike's glove.

That spring Willie's fastball had lost its zip. He'd won only two games, the team just three. Mike had been in a hitting slump all season. The battery duds, some of the team thought, but never said so because Willie and Mike would wait for them after practice, somewhere away from school property.

Earlier that afternoon the team had lost again. "You'd think she might at least have come to the last game of the season," Mike said. "She doesn't like baseball," Willie answered. "What does she like?" Mike asked. "I invited her for a boat ride and she didn't say no," Willie replied. "Three's company, right?" Mike said. "Yeah, I'm going to need you, man. Going to be fog," Willie said.

Nicki waited to make sure Willie didn't turn around and drive back to talk to her. She wouldn't have agreed to the boat ride, but her mother had more or less asked her to accept for the tenuous reason that Wesley Boots and Sheldon Groh were business partners and accepting Willie's invitation would be a sociable thing to do.

Willie's car disappeared at the curve where Main Street divides, one road going toward the shopping center and the other dropping down to the lake. Nicki walked around the building to the parking lot behind the bookstore. The man in the car had been grading papers while he waited for her. He picked up the finished ones scattered across the passenger seat. The Miata was black, and hard to see into if you were standing outside or coming out the back door of the real estate agency that shared the parking lot with the bookstore. No one could see Nicki and the man kissing.

The man's name was Francis Hennesy. His middle initial was X. He was twenty-three and had been teaching math at the high school for a year. The students called him the X-man. X, you're done for, the students said, drawing their fingers across their throats, stricken. He was considered a tough teacher. Nicki called him Fran.

Nicki was almost nineteen. She had fallen for Fran the first moment she saw him. He's beautiful, Nicki told her mother, and described Mr. Hennesy's blond hair, blue eyes, and wide shoulders.

Weekends Nicki and a couple of girls in her class usually drove to Hanover for Indian or Thai food. They bought tickets to performances at the Hop across the street from the Dartmouth campus. Nicki and her friends didn't spend much time in Jeffrey, which didn't even have a movie theater anymore, and where most of the town's events took place on the green in summer when Jeffrey was filled with visitors.

Nicki's awareness of Mr. Hennesy pleased Harriet. She assumed Nicki's attraction to him would find its way to a classmate, or a college student perhaps. Harriet was fairly certain Nicki had crashed some Dartmouth parties. Harriet also assumed that Nicki might catch up with the daughters that Harriet's friends talked about, daughters they had made doctors' appointments for, whose prescriptions were refilled without comment. A few weeks after school started and Nicki had seen Mr. Hennesy, Nicki had made her own appointment. When Harriet glimpsed the pink pill case in Nicki's drawer, she was not surprised. Harriet did not, however, pass on the information to Sheldon. Though Nicki was their daughter, there was something private about what Harriet had found, something Sheldon did not need to know.

Adopting had been Harriet's idea. Sheldon wanted to keep trying. Harriet knew better. Harriet apologized to Sheldon for her *inadequacy,* her word, but she knew it was the one Sheldon would choose himself. Her female anatomy was imperfect, she explained. Well, let's adopt then, Sheldon said. His sounded weary of the whole subject. Except for the forms he had to fill out and the interviews he had to participate in, he left matters in Harriet's hands. Two years later, Harriet said there was a child named Nicki who was available. Sheldon was not prepared for a frail child who had been neglected and abused in foster homes, who stumbled, who vomited, who squatted in the yard to relieve herself. But he was patient with her, gentle, though always distant.

Harriet was not surprised to find the pink container designed to dispense one tiny pill for each numbered day, but she was disappointed because she and Nicki had always been close and open with each other, a little sad that Nicki had not spoken to her first, had not said this is what I've decided to do and the two of them then doing it together. Nor would Nicki say whom she was seeing. Harriet never suspected Francis Hennesy.

In January, before school vacation ended, when the crews had cleared the roads from the recent snow, Nicki asked, Can I bring you anything from Boston?

"When?" Harriet asked.

"Tomorrow," Nicki said. "Fran is driving."

"Fran?"

"Mr. Hennesy," Nicki said.

"The math teacher?" Harriet asked, and sat down, questions suddenly spinning in her mind.

"We're meeting his brother," Nicki said.

Harriet had seen Fran, Mr. Hennesy, eating lunch at the coffee shop on Main Street one Saturday when Harriet and Ruth Lindsay had stopped in for espresso. Ruth was on the school board, as was Sheldon. Ruth pointed out Fran. Definitely handsome. I doubt we can keep him, Ruth said.

"Could you be a bit more specific?" Harriet asked.

"I don't know. I've never met Fran's brother."

"How well do you know Mr. Hennesy? You call him Fran."

"The school doesn't mind first names."

"But the school would mind if someone saw you together in Boston."

"Mom, Fran's brother works for a biotech company. There's a possibility for a summer internship."

"Oh . . ." Harriet took a deep breath. The questions weren't so important after all. "You couldn't commute to Boston every day," Harriet said.

"The company's in Andover. That's less than an hour."

"Then I hope it works out."

Questions answered. A pause. Nicki wasn't finished.

"Mom, how much more do you want to hear?"

"I'm listening," Harriet said.

"Fran and I have been seeing each other. Since November."

Harriet was still sitting. She reached out and Nicki took her hand. Harriet kissed it and pressed it against her cheek.

"Does anyone else know?" Harriet asked.

"No one."

"How have you managed?"

"Fran rents a house in Springfield. It's very private."

Harriet realized she didn't want to find out anything else, at least not right now. She continued to hold Nicki's hand. If she let go, Nicki would drift away, or she would.

"Mom, you okay?"

"If you're happy, I'm okay." Harriet looked into Nicki's eyes and saw she was happy. "Okay and concerned," Harriet said, not quite ready to pretend she had accepted Nicki's news as if she and Nicki were not mother and daughter, not ready at all to let the drifting apart begin.

In the weeks following, Harriet sometimes found herself a bit envious of Nicki, in whose face, when she returned around seven for supper, Harriet saw the lingering glow of pleasure. At other times, Harriet fretted that the risk of discovery made the relationship too intense for someone Nicki's age. Harriet found herself wishing Nicki would have . . . what did one call a casual physical relationship now? . . . that sort of relationship, whatever it was called, with a man her own age, a boy.

So when Sheldon said wouldn't it be nice if Nicki and Willie Boots saw something of each other, even though Harriet knew that Sheldon was asking for Nicki to do him a favor and accept an invitation from Willie, the son of Sheldon's business partner, and even though Harriet had no fondness for Willie, whom she had watched grow up to worship his mistaken self-image of athletic beauty and irresistibility, she agreed with Sheldon. Harriet talked to Nicki, who said yes when Willie invited her to come along on the boat.

Nicki leaned over and rested her cheek against Fran's leg. He lifted her hair between his fingers, softly let it fall. No one had ever seen them touching, not even Kevin, Fran's brother, who had been impressed by how much science Nicki knew and had arranged for the internship.

You seduced me, didn't you? Fran had said one November afternoon. The leaves had fallen. By five o'clock the sky was almost dark. November was not Fran's favorite month, but this one was different. Darkness and cold and bare trees didn't mean much anymore. Nicki pushed them out of his mind.

Put a spell on, not seduced, she preferred to think; led him every step of the way from politeness to curiosity to bewilderment to infatuation. Most of all to trust. She made him know she desired him, convinced him she would not betray him. One word to her friends, to anyone really, would be a word turned into many words, many whisperings that would reach the wrong ears, rumors that would need sorting out. Fran would be dismissed. The press would be at his door.

Fran felt uneasy about Willie and Mike. In the faculty lounge other teachers often mentioned them. They're sneaky, someone said. Just clever enough not to get caught, someone else said. Caught at what? Fran wondered. Bad citizens, another teacher said. But Fran didn't tell Nicki what other teachers thought because that would be teacher to student and that was not what they were to each other. Nevertheless, Nicki sensed Fran's discomfort with her decision to accept Willie's invitation.

"You're sweet to worry," Nicki said. "But I'll be all right." She kissed Fran again, brushed her hair, smoothed her skirt. "I'll see you tomorrow."

Fran watched Nicki walk past the bookstore toward the street. Tomorrow he'd shop in the morning, buy some flowers for the table by the bed, buy something to eat. Nicki would arrive at his house around noon. They would drink wine and prepare a complicated salad, eat it with a loaf of crusty bread from the new bread shop in town. They would drink more wine and go to bed and make love and nap and make love again. Then the afternoon would be gone. Nicki would go home. He'd probably finish grading the rest of his papers. Sunday he might see her again. He realized he was beginning to shape his days around hers, his future too. He hadn't told her, but he had applied for a teaching job at a prep school in New Jersey, a half hour from Princeton, where she would start her freshman year in September. They could go to restaurants together, go anywhere, be seen together. No one would care.

He hadn't heard about the job yet, so he hadn't said anything about it to Nicki. She was strange in one way, she never talked about the future. She never seemed to plan more than a few days ahead. She never talked about Princeton, or what she was going to study, or what one day she'd like to be. She didn't talk about the past either. I'm adopted, that's all she said. The scars on her legs where she'd been burned, they happened in foster care was her only comment. Even if Fran got the job, he didn't know when he would tell her.

"Willie's a good boy," Sheldon commented over supper. "Get to know him. He's smart like his dad."

Nicki knew that her father and Wesley Boots had grown up together. After college they'd both returned to Jeffrey, Sheldon to work in his father's hardware business, Wesley Boots to work for his father too, a man who owned property, including the ski area on Mount Blue. After Sheldon's father died, Sheldon sold the hardware business and became Wesley's partner. On farm land the Boots family owned, Wesley and Sheldon built houses. At the edge of town, they built a shopping center. On the mountain, they built condominiums. Now they were constructing a conference center between Jeffrey and Hanover.

Nicki knew that Sheldon Groh needed Wesley Boots. Wesley had seen more potential in Sheldon than others had. The Grohs were wealthy because of Wesley Boots. What Nicki had a hard time understanding was the relationship between her parents. If love was politeness and civility, then they were in love. If love involved passion, she could not imagine her parents in love. Yes, they slept in the same bed, but they did not seem to need each other. Yes, they kissed, they touched. They didn't not fondle, they did not press against each other, they did not seem to want to taste each other. They did not miss each other. Perhaps fondling and tasting were what young lovers did, what she and Fran did, yet Nicki glimpsed in her parents' eyes no look of melancholy, no sorrow for a passion lost but not forgotten. Sometimes Nicki wondered if they had chosen each other they way they had chosen her. She was available to them, they were available to each other. But that idea was cold and left Nicki feeling guilty. She loved her mother. She did not love her father, but she was grateful to him.

Willie arrived at eight to pick up Nicki. The scene in the hall, Willie shaking hands with Sheldon, calling him sir, gave Harriet hope that Willie was the good kid Sheldon said he was, and that Nicki might have a good time.

Mike was lying down on the backseat of Willie's yellow Jeep. He rose when Willie opened the door.

"Definitely fog, like you said," Mike mumbled and slid down again.

"I'm a weather expert," Willie informed Nicki.

The Boots house was built up the hill overlooking the lake, the boathouse across the road. Willie parked the Jeep at the boathouse. Mike handed Willie two six-packs of beer.

A boardwalk led to the boathouse, which was taken apart and stored every winter. The lake had been free of ice for two weeks now. Willie turned on the lights. The boat was long and sleek, the name *Lady of the Lake* written in gold letters on the stern. Willie said the boat was real wood and worth a lot of money.

Willie climbed in. Nicki followed. She could feel him watching her, how her sweater revealed the shape of a breast when she brushed back her hair, how her jeans revealed her hips when she bent over. Mike walked around the boat unknotting the ropes. Then he jumped into the boat. Willie started the motor, sending up a cloud of exhaust. In a minute the boat was cruising down the middle of the lake. Although the lake was the reason tourists filled the town every summer, Nicki had never been on the water. She preferred hiking to swimming and boating. She looked at the houses going by in the darkness. Only a few lights were on.

Mike opened three beers. Corona. Nicki liked the taste. She also liked the chill of the wind on her skin. Willie and Mike had on T-shirts that showed off their muscles and the tattoos around their biceps.

Mike uncapped a second beer and lit a joint. He passed it to Nicki. Just a little smoke, she thought. The wind on her skin felt soft and dark.

"Having a good time?" Willie asked.

"It's nice here," Nicki said.

"It gets better," Willie said.

Mike stood on the other side of Nicki. Fog was beginning to hover above the water. "You called it," Mike said. There was still enough moonlight for Nicki to see the silhouettes of empty houses and a few boats anchored near the shore.

"Want a tour?" Willie asked.

"Sure," Nicki said.

Mike moved over to the wheel. Willie offered Nicki another beer. "I'm fine," she said. She noticed Willie look at Mike and grin.

Nicki followed Willie down steep, narrow steps. The air was stale, the hum of the motor louder.

A galley, then bunks along each side of the hull, and a bathroom—the head—Willie called it. Willie put his arm around her and kissed her lightly on the mouth. His skin smelled like a cologne ad. She tried to turn away. He kissed her again. There wasn't much room to move in. His hand caressed her back, then drifted down and pressed her hips into his. She could feel him through his pants. "Let's go back," she said.

"No, let's sit down," he said. He pushed her toward one of the bunks. "Relax," he said.

She leaned against the bulkhead and pulled her legs toward her chest. Willie sat on the bunk and faced her. He had almost finished his beer. He leaned forward and slipped his hand between her legs.

"I give good massages," he said.

"No thanks," Nicki said.

Willie's fingers worked up her legs.

"What are you doing?" Nicki asked.

"Feeling what a great body you have," Willie said.

Nicki sensed the boat change direction. The motor grew muffled.

"Stand up," Willie said.

Nicki stood up. Willie pressed himself against her. "I've got a great body too," he said.

Nicki turned and started to walk away. Willie pulled her back, his hands spread on her thighs. He moved his hands higher. He nuzzled her neck. He licked her skin. She couldn't move. He raised the hem of her sweater. She tried to turn around. His other arm was locked around her chest. His hand slipped between her skin and her jeans. His fingers played over her underwear.

"No," she said. Her hand gripped his and tried to pry it away.

The door to the deck opened. Mike stood on the steps.

"Okay," Willie said. He freed his arm and gave Nicki a push in Mike's direction. "The lady says no," Willie said.

Mike turned around. Nicki followed him up the steps. She could hardly see past the running lights on the bow.

Willie said. "Think it's swim time?"

"Yes, I do. Most definitely I do," Mike said.

Willie's arms encircled Nicki again. He dragged her toward the side. She tried to grab something to hold on to. Mike's arms lifted her legs off the deck. Air rushed by. Water smacked her face. Cold took her breath away.

She gasped for air. Water soaked her jeans, weighted her down. Willie leaned over the side watching. Her hand reached for the hull and slid off.

The motor churned the water. The boat moved away. Stopped. Willie cast a ladder over the side. She struggled toward it. The boat moved away again. She swam after it again, hands slapping against the water. She had no breath to yell, none to use to cry out, barely enough to swim at all. She hauled herself up and flopped onto the deck and lay there coughing and spitting. Willie stood over her. She squinted at the thick rubber soles of his shoes.

"Change your mind?" Willie asked.

She got her weight under her and lunged at him. He jumped, spilling beer on the deck.

"Guess not," he said.

Mike seized her shoulders. His knees pinned her against the deck. Willie unsnapped her jeans. She kicked at him. The jeans soon tangled around her feet. The deck burned her skin. Willie yanked off her jeans.

"Easier to swim this way," he said.

Willie and Mike dragged Nicki to the side and dumped her overboard again. The motor rumbled. The boat moved away, farther than before. It was hard to see the ladder in the fog.

Instead of swimming toward the boat, Nicki began to swim away from it. Her legs were free now. She kicked her feet and turned onto her back. The boat disappeared. She kept swimming. Finally she put her feet down. They touched slippery stones. She waded toward the shore.

There was no beach. The trees leaned over the water. She clung to a branch and pulled herself onto land. She stood and listened. She heard a radio.

The fog was more over the water than the land. The light from a waning moon paled the leaves. She zigzagged through the trees, going from branch to branch to keep her balance. Rocks cut her feet. The music grew louder. Light shimmered in a clearing. She made out the headlamps of a car, and a man standing by the door listening to a country song.

His eyes opened wide. He beheld a woman staggering out of the trees. A soggy sweater covered her chest. Twisted underpants clung to her body. She shivered.

He held out a blanket. She was shivering so much she could not raise her arms. She pressed them tightly against herself. He wrapped the blanket around her and knew it was not enough. He took off his own sweater and put it around her, but that was not enough. He led her to the car and helped her into it. He closed the doors and turned on the heater and pressed her in the blanket against his chest.

Nicki stopped shivering. Slowly the man let go of her. She couldn't remember his name, but he'd been in a class with her. Two years ago. Maybe three.

"I'm Nicki," she said.

"I know," he said. "I'm Russell."

"Russ Blatt," she said. "Earth science class."

"I prefer Russell."

"Sorry."

"It's okay."

"Where are we?"

"The poor part of the lake."

"I don't know the lake."

"This is a cove that isn't interesting enough for the summer people to want to buy."

"Where's your house?"

"About a half mile toward the road."

"What are you doing here?"

"What are you doing here?"

"There was some trouble on a boat."

"I'm here getting ready to leave." He pointed at some cans of motor oil. "You need a doctor?"

"Can you drive me home?"

"I have to put oil in first. I have clothes too. Maybe you better put some on."

Russell opened one of the boxes on the backseat and gave Nicki sweatpants, a shirt, and wool socks.

Nicki felt as if she'd had a fever and her muscles wouldn't work anymore. Russell helped her out of the car and folded back the blanket. He drew the sweater over Nicki's head and snugged the shirt around her.

The air was cold and Nicki began to shiver again. "Take off everything wet," Russell said. Nicki reached under the shirt and unfastened her bra. He turned Nicki around, her back toward him, the blanket between them. She pushed her underpants down her legs and pulled on the warm sweatpants.

"I'll finish up," Russell said.

He opened the cans and poured the oil. "The car's old, but it's in good shape," he said.

"What did you mean, you're getting ready to leave?" Nicki asked.

"Leave New Hampshire."

"I'm going in the fall," Nicki said.

"College?"

Nicki nodded. "What about you?"

"No college."

"Where are you going?"

"South."

"Where south?"

"Wherever looks good."

"You can just do that?"

"Sure. Why not?"

"I don't know. I never thought about it."

Russell wiped his hands on a rag and stored the empty cans in a box in the trunk of the car. Nicki got in and Russell started the engine. She saw several old boats abandoned in the weeds. A chain stretched across the path. Russell let down the chain, backed the car onto the road, then locked the chain in place again. Down the road Nicki saw a trailer. A light was on. She saw a truck parked outside with pieces of pipe on the roof.

She started to tell Russell where she lived. He said he knew.

"Where do you live?" she asked.

"We just passed it," he said.

Russell drove into town. On Main Street he turned onto Pleasant and stopped. A block away Nicki saw Wesley Boots's Mercedes in front of her house.

"You okay?" Russell asked.

"Depends on whose version you hear," Nicki said.

Russell waited. "Go ahead," she said. "Let's get this over with."

Russell parked behind the Mercedes. "Look," Nicki said, "when are you leaving? I want to give your clothes back."

"Tomorrow. My dad goes to work about nine. I'll probably leave around ten."

"What's your number? I'll call you at nine-thirty," Nicki said.

Nicki closed the door softly and watched Russell drive away. She walked through the yard and up the back steps. When she came into the kitchen, her mother, her father, Willie, and Wesley Boots spun around.

"Oh, thank God," Harriet said and rushed to put her arms around Nicki. Her father and Wesley Boots stood there watching.

"Okay then. Safe and sound," Wesley Boots said. He nudged Willie toward the door. Willie might have said something in the hall, but the men spoke in low voices and Nicki couldn't understand them.

"You scared the hell out of us," her father said.

Nicki was sitting down at the kitchen table now. "I was scared too," she said.

"We partied our senior year. I guess I understand, but the water thing . . . well, we were about to call the deputy. That's how concerned we were."

"Is that what Willie told you? We partied?"

"Partied too much. He apologized for bringing the beer. He said he didn't realize how many you drank."

"I drank too much beer and what . . . what did he say?"

"You fell overboard and started swimming."

"That was a dumb thing to do." Sheldon didn't respond to Nicki's sarcasm.

"Under the circumstances, when Willie and Mike are trying to get you back in the boat, yes, it was a dumb thing to do."

Harriet caressed Nicki's shoulders. "Sheldon, it's not important now," she said.

"Right. You're here, you're safe, that's what's important. How did you get home?"

"I swam to shore and someone gave me a ride."

"And some clothes obviously. This person have a name?"

"Sheldon, can't this wait?"

Her father filled a glass with ice and poured whiskey into it. He swallowed and leaned against the counter. "I guess so," he said.

"Sweetie, get into bed. I'll be up in a minute," Harriet said.

"I want to shower first," Nicki answered.

Nicki stood under the hot spray until her mother knocked. Nicki wrapped herself in a towel. Her mother came in and closed the door.

"Nicki, what happened?"

"Willie wanted to have sex. I didn't. I ended up in the water."

"Ended up?"

"Willie and Mike threw me in."

"They didn't . . . ?"

"No, they didn't."

"But they tried?"

"Willie did."

"You were both drinking?"

"Does that matter?"

"I'm sorry. Of course it doesn't. It's just . . ."

"Things happen, you mean?"

"Yes. Things happen. Especially at your age when you're drinking."

"There's no point in saying anything to Dad, is there?"

"I will if you want me to."

Nicki shook her head.

Harriet put her arms around Nicki. "Sweetie, I'm so sorry. But I'm thankful you're all right. You are, aren't you?"

"I'm a little shaky, that's all. And angry. The money Dad is going to pay Princeton, Mr. Boots helped him get it."

"Helped him earn it."

"I don't want to use it."

"Sweetie, now isn't the best time to make decisions. We'll talk tomorrow. Okay?"

"Tomorrow," Nicki said.

It was already tomorrow. Nicki lay in bed and thought about Russell leaving. At nine-thirty she'd phone and ask him to wait.

II

Nicki asked Russell to stay until Monday. She said she wanted to go with him. She would miss her graduation on Tuesday.

She was standing outside the gym at the college, a blue athletic bag at her feet. In it, three hundred dollars, withdrawn that morning from the ATM machine, and as many clothes as the bag would hold. Thanks for waiting, she said. She leaned against the seat and closed her eyes. From time to time she wiped her cheeks. Russell thought she'd change her mind before they reached the Massachusetts border, but she didn't.

The car was an Olds Cutlass, Russell said. It was big and comfortable. They ate when they stopped for gas. They took turns driving and sleeping in the backseat.

They were sitting at a picnic table. The air was hot, pungent with pine resin and the smell of charred cardboard from the trash can close by. Russell unwrapped a cheese sandwich. A bee buzzed his Pepsi can. Nicki ate a banana and drank a bottle of water.

"You disappeared. Did you change schools?" Nicki asked.

"Homeschool," Russell said and laughed.

"What's funny?"

"I sent to the state for the forms for homeschooling and filled them out and signed my father's name. No one ever checked up."

"What about your father?"

"As long as I cooked his supper, kept his rum glass full, woke him up in the morning, and fed him breakfast, he didn't care what I did."

"What did you do?"

"Mornings I hung out at the college library and read books. In the afternoon, I helped a woman who lived by herself. I did her shopping and took her to doctor's appointments. The car was her husband's. She gave it to me. She died in April."

"Did you tell your father you were going?"

"No. You tell yours?"

"No."

"Tell your mom?"

"I called her."

"What did you say?"

"I said I'd be all right and I was going with someone I knew. I promised I'd phone her again."

"She ask you why you were going?"

"She knows."

Russell poured a pool of Pepsi on the table for the bee.

"What kind of books did you read?"

"Poetry mostly. Spanish poetry."

"You have Mr. Mendoza in Spanish?"

"Second year. He was a good teacher."

"Think they should have fired him?"

"No, but the minute he said what he was, he should have known they would."

"If you were a gay teacher, you wouldn't tell anyone?"

"Even if I wasn't a teacher, I'd be careful who I told."

"Would you tell me?"

"If you needed to know."

"Are you?"

"Do you need to know?"

"Not that much."

The bee walked around the Pepsi, not quite sure what to do with it.

"Who was in the boat with you?" Russell asked.

"Willie Boots and Mike Hastings."

"I remember them. They sprayed *fag* on Mr. Mendoza's windshield. Except the 'a' looked like an 'o.'

[208]

The next day he said he told his students he drove home looking through *fog*. I thought that was funny. Showed more class than Willie and Mike ever could."

The bee flew off. "I'll try Mountain Dew next time," Russell said. He overhanded the can and the sandwich wrapper at the trash barrel.

In the car he opened a package of cigarettes. "Let me have one," Nicki said. He leaned closer to her to light it. He studied her mouth. Women's mouths were soft with forgiveness.

"What happened?" Sheldon said. "I mean Nicki didn't have a lot of friends, but she wasn't in trouble. Not much interested in boys, maybe. I don't know. Good student. Then one day she's gone. Run off. Didn't even go to her own graduation. I bet people have plenty to say about us."

"People feel concerned for us."

"People feel we owe them an explanation. I'd give them one if I had one."

"You feel I owe you an explanation?"

"You're taking things pretty calmly, under the circumstances."

"Sheldon, I love Nicki and I'm very worried about her. But she sounded okay. She sounded like she knew what she was doing. She promised to call again."

"But why is she doing what she's doing and who is she doing it with?"

"I don't know who she left with, but I think she needs some space."

"'Some space?' What the hell does that mean?"

"Perspective. Nicki wants to put things that have happened into perspective."

"Like what she did on the boat?"

"There may be other things."

"I certainly get some strange looks. As if we did something."

"Maybe we did."

"Like what? Like giving her a good home, opportunities, clothes, education? Princeton? We gave her Princeton, for God's sake."

"I wouldn't count on her going to Princeton now."

"I'm not counting on anything now. I'm not even counting on ever seeing her again."

"I am, Sheldon. I'm counting on it very much."

He had almost said that maybe not seeing Nicki wouldn't be such a bad thing, but he didn't. When he spoke with Wesley Boots the next day, he asked if he had ever hired a detective. No, Wesley said, adding that there were detectives listed in the Yellow Pages of the Concord phone book.

In North Carolina, Russell left the interstate. He took a winding mountain road and stopped for gas in Wireville.

"I want to eat in a restaurant," Nicki said. She pointed to the Cotton Café across the street. They left the car under a shade tree.

Nicki ordered the trout special. Russell asked for a hamburger and a beer. The waitress looked at his I.D. and okayed it.

"You twenty-one?" Nicki whispered.

"Course not," he said.

The waitress brought Russell's beer and Nicki's unsweetened tea. "Are you visiting or passing through?" she asked.

"Would this be a good place to visit?" Russell answered.

"The spa of the Smokies," she said.

She brought their meals and handed Nicki a brochure with pictures of nearby Laurel Lake. Besides private cabins for rent, there was Laurel Lodge. "A nice place. Real popular in the summer," she said. "Lots of Florida people come here to beat the heat."

Nicki ordered a cobbler for dessert. The waitress laid the bill on the table and watched Nicki and Russell count out their money. "You're not lookin' for work, are you?"

"Are we?" Nicki asked.

"I think it's a good idea," Russell said.

The waitress introduced herself. "I'm Bonnie. My sister Betty manages the lodge. She needs help bad." Bonnie said she'd phone her sister and tell her Nicki and Russell were on their way.

"What can you do?" Russell asked.

"I made sandwiches last summer at the café," Nicki said.

Russell drove the Cutlass past a stone gatepost and parked in front of a log building with green shutters and rocking chairs on the wide porch.

Betty greeted them at the reception desk and explained she needed waitstaff and someone to work in housekeeping to inspect rooms, making sure the housekeepers had done everything right, and to check out complaints.

"You don't speak Spanish, by any chance?"

"I know a little," Russell said.

"You just earned a raise," Betty said. "No one around here speaks Spanish but half the staff does."

Nicki and Russell filled out employment forms and promised to work through Labor Day.

"There's one double left in Baily. That's were the staff bunks," Betty said.

Two weeks had passed since Nicki called. Sometimes Harriet was angry that Nicki hadn't phoned again. Sometimes she was merely resigned. Either way, Nicki filled her thoughts. So did Francis Hennesy. Had Nicki phoned him? Did he know more than she knew? Enough of pretending she didn't know about Nicki and Fran. Harriet found his address.

The small Cape stood in a meadow at the end of a gravel road. Harriet didn't see a car. She walked around and peered in the windows. Rooms uncluttered and bright with sunlight.

At the back of the house Harriet discovered a deck. Some flowers and herbs grew in pots. Harriet leaned against the railing and stared into the woods. Through the trees a pond glimmered among shadows.

The screen door was unlocked. A cup and a plate were drying in the dish rack. A tea towel was neatly folded on the counter. She picked up the letter from the table and read it. A school in New Jersey was offering Fran a job. Was that the plan? He was going where she was going? Had Nicki changed her mind? Was she running away from Fran too? Some answers, please. Some answers.

But there weren't any. Harriet returned to her car. Then she saw the black Miata approaching the house.

"You're Nicki's mother, aren't you?" Fran said.

It crossed Harriet's mind to answer, And you're Nicki's lover. "Please call me Harriet," she said, and shook the hand he offered her.

"Coffee, if you're making some," Harriet said, after he had asked as she stood in the kitchen watching him put away his groceries.

"No trouble," Fran answered.

"Have you heard from Nicki?"

"She phoned. She said she'd told you about us. She wondered if you might come over."

"Here I am."

"Here we both are," Fran said.

"When did she phone?"

"The day she left. She called me before she called you. I thought that meant something in my favor. Later on I realized I was probably easier for her to talk to. I mean . . ."

"I know what you mean."

Fran ground the coffee. A wisp of steam rose from the pot on the stove.

"Did Nicki say anything to you at all, before she left?"

"Not in so many words."

Harriet watched Fran pour the water over the coffee. He seemed to move in slow motion, his back toward her.

"Tell me," Harriet said.

"She was different. Distant, distracted. Quiet. Something had happened. She didn't say what."

"She went on a boat ride with Willie Boots. She wouldn't have sex with him. Willie and his friend Mike threw her into the lake. She ended up swimming to shore."

Fran slumped against the counter and shook his head. Finally he pushed himself up. He poured the coffee into two mugs and set out spoons, milk, and sugar.

"Willie's father's really the problem. He and my husband are business partners. Mr. Boots came to the house before Nicki got home. My husband believes Willie's version of what happened. She'd been drinking and fell overboard."

"Nicki told me she and her father aren't close."

"Nicki wasn't what Sheldon had in mind. He wasn't unkind to her. But they're not close."

"He doesn't believe her either?"

"Nicki didn't tell him."

They were sitting at the table. Fran tucked the letter under his mug.

"Princeton's the other thing," Harriet said. "Nicki doesn't want her tuition paid with money Wesley Boots helped my husband earn."

"Thanks for telling me," Fran said.

"I snooped. I read the letter. I'm sorry."

"Don't apologize. Right now if there's an offer, I wouldn't know what to do."

What Harriet wanted to know was what she should do. But she didn't think Fran could tell her. She pushed her mug toward the center of the table and stood up.

"Call me if you hear from Nicki, please," Harriet said.

Fran walked her to her car. He stood very close to her, as if he might hug her, comfort her. But he was scarcely older than Nicki. She should hug him. "I'll call," he said.

"Pay attention," Betty said, handing Nicki the tray.

"You figured how to load and unload, but you're too stiff. You got to be firm and flexible at the same time. And when you're carrying a cocktail like a straight-up martini, or even a cup of coffee, never ever look at what you're carrying. You do and you'll spill for sure. Third thing, spend a little longer with your tables. You're taking orders too fast. Talk a bit. Be sweet, especially to the older ones. The kitchen can't keep up with you. You got to work with its rhythm, not the other way around. Okay?"

Nicki would finish around ten. Her legs and shoulders ached. Russell massaged her shoulders while they sat watching the night sky deepen, the stars brighten. *Mientras la tierra sueña solitaria, vela la blanca luna,* he recited. While the earth sleeps alone, the white moon keeps watch, he said when she asked him what it meant.

They slept in twin beds with a small table and a lamp on it between them. They took turns dressing and undressing in the bathroom at the end of the hall. Do my legs too, Nicki said one night. She had returned from the bathroom wearing a thin shirt that fell to her hips. She lay on her stomach. Russell knelt over her and started with her calves, working gently at first, warming the muscle, then deeper.

Turn over, he said. He slicked his palms with baby oil. Nicki's shirt was bunched around her waist. His hands worked up her thighs. She covered her eyes with her arm, giving him privacy to stare at the shadow beneath her underwear. She wanted him to want her. She wanted him to make her less lonely. He had told her the story. His father had been called to fix the plumbing at the Twilight Villas and saw Russell going into one of the cabins with an older man. Russell could try, couldn't he? Her desire shamed her. That's enough, she said and drew the sheet over her legs.

"When you adopt someone, you never really know," Sheldon said. "You always wonder if there's a problem, something tucked away and one day it'll go off."

"Something did?"

"She did, for sure."

"And you have no idea who she went with?"

"Absolutely none. Neither her mother nor I have a clue."

"I'll find her. That's what you pay me for."

"Her mother doesn't know anything about this. If you do locate her, you tell me."

"I'll be in touch," the man said. Sheldon watched the detective's black Trans Am pass a front-loader carrying pipe. Dust hung in the air. July had been a dry month.

"There's hardly enough water for swimming," Fran said. It was the third time Harriet had driven out to tell him she had heard from Nicki again. No, it was the third time she had driven out to talk to someone about Nicki. When Harriet and Fran talked, Nicki felt more real to Harriet than she did when she called. The phone conversations were short, insubstantial, frustrating. Hi, Mom. I'm okay. I miss you. I'm not ready to come home yet. Don't ask where I am. Don't worry. I'm really all right.

Harriet and Fran stood under the pines. The sun on the float in the center of the pond turned the wood into something soft and warm-looking.

"Usually you have to swim to it, but this summer you can wade," Fran said.

Harriet had on a modest tennis outfit with a flared skirt that passed the dress code at the country club. She hadn't played with anyone. For an hour she had hit balls against the backboard.

Harriet unlaced her sneakers and left them on the shore. The rocks were slippery. She held on to Fran's hand. Fran jogged every morning. He had put on a dry shirt. His shorts were split up the side, showing how tan he was. Harriet supposed if he was there alone he'd take off his clothes. Thinking about it bothered her, his body's sudden vividness.

She sat next to Fran on the edge of the float. When he moved his legs back and forth in the water, a tiny current tingled her skin. A dragonfly hovered overhead, its blue body reminding her of the color of her mother's Wedgwood teacups.

"When Nicki does come home," Fran said, "I think I shouldn't be here."

"I don't understand," Harriet said.

"She won't come back until it's on her own terms."

"I still don't understand about you."

"Nicki started our relationship. She wouldn't let me say no. She knew the trouble it might cause, but she knew she was worth it. What happened with Willie changed how she felt about things. I'm not saying she felt differently about herself. She thought differently about me. When she came here the next day, I expected things to be the way they were before. We made love because I expected it. She was giving in, but she didn't believe in it anymore."

Why the flutter of her heart when Harriet heard Fran say he and Nicki made love? Certainly Harriet knew what they did. But she was blushing. She bent over to hide it.

"She'll change back," Harriet said.

"With someone else."

"Do you miss her?"

"I miss talking to her."

"What would you say to her if she were here now?"

"It doesn't matter if a good priest or a bad priest administers a sacrament. It works either way."

"You mean money's money.

"She should use it to go to Princeton."

"Are you Catholic?"

"My mother was."

"I don't think Princeton's going to happen."

"I don't either."

"What about you?"

"I'm leaving in September. Tell Nicki you read in the paper I resigned from the high school."

Harriet stared at the water for a while, then she reached out and laid her hand on Fran's arm. "I'll miss talking to you," she said. *I kept looking at the water, feeling his hand on mine. Not all our moments were about Nicki. We had searched each other with our eyes, gone over each other part by part. And the way he had told me to tell her that I'd read it in the paper, so I wouldn't have to admit I had been coming to his house. His mouth vivid in my mind now. Was mine vivid in his? Please, it's so easy for people to make each other disappear.*

Harriet moved her hand. "I need to start back," she said.

Harriet slid off the side into the water. Looking toward the trees, she held on to the float a second to feel the bottom. She walked slowly, a woman with the sun on her shoulders, a woman aware she was still attractive and knowing a man was watching her.

Russell woke. Nicki was softly crying in her bed, her arm across her face, like the time when he had massaged her legs. She hadn't asked him to do that again. He watched her, unsure what to do now, but he knew the feeling of wanting someone to hold you, the feeling that only the touch of that person could make you real.

He eased his body down beside hers. Her eyes flew open, her arm ready to push him away. Then she recognized his face in the dark and lifted the sheet and put her arms around him and held him tightly against her, warming his body with her heat, wetting his cheek with her tears.

After a while she stopped crying and pushed down the sheet to let the air cool her skin. Russell raised the hem of her shirt and wiped her face. "It's okay, you don't have to," she said.

"Wireville, North Carolina. Your daughter works at a place called Laurel Lodge," the detective said.

"How did you find her?"

"She's phoned your house from there."

Sheldon knew the man was saying, Buddy, you're really out of it.

"Is she with anyone?" Sheldon asked.

"You didn't pay me to find that out."

"My daughter had a cell phone. Can you get a record of the calls she made?"

"Easy."

"It was a Christmas present. Who she called between January and May. Find out if there's anyone she called a lot."

"No problem," the detective said.

Sheldon usually ate a sandwich for lunch at the café on Main Street. Today he decided on the inn. Jimmy made a good whiskey sour. Sheldon sipped his cocktail and wondered if Harriet had known all along where Nicki was. Okay if she did; okay if she didn't. It was who Nicki went away with that interested Sheldon. He was sure Harriet didn't know who, and he was sure if he found out he would understand why Nicki had gone away.

Sometimes you get to a point when you know things are all going to go wrong and you don't care, you let it happen. I knew it when I was driving toward Fran's house and Sheldon was leaving. I couldn't turn around. I couldn't make myself vanish. Sheldon stopped beside me. A puff of dust rose up behind his car. I imagined it was one of those thought balloons hovering above a character's head in a cartoon. This one was blank. We could have reached out our windows and touched each other. We didn't. I wondered if I appeared as baffled as he was. Then it crossed my mind that Sheldon was on the school board and maybe he had driven out to try to talk Fran into staying at the school. What crossed his mind? And what could I tell him, how could I explain? Well, you see, Fran and our daughter were lovers. Quite naturally I thought maybe he'd heard from her. That would have been a lie, though. I wasn't there to talk about Nicki. I was there to talk about myself. I was wearing a new dress, a little more revealing than what I usually wear, and slingbacks I kept looking down to admire, the way a girl does her first heels. I felt girlish too. I had painted my nails a deep red.

Sheldon didn't say anything. He shook his head and drove off. I was sure he had me in his mirror. Let things go where they want to go, I thought. I'm very popular with the Groh family today, Fran said. He poured me a lemonade and we sat on the deck. I could have used something stronger. Nicki often phoned Fran, Sheldon had found out. He didn't say how, but I guessed. Fran said the calls were about his brother and the internship. Not very honest of me, was it? Fran said. Then Sheldon had wanted to know if Fran had any idea who Nicki was seeing, who she might have gone away with. Fran said that everyone in Nicki's class was present and accounted for at graduation, everyone except Nicki. So Sheldon decided it was someone who wasn't in school anymore, or maybe someone from Hanover.

What are you going to say? Fran asked. It depends, I said, on what Sheldon asks me. But I saw the opportunities for cover. I could have driven out to ask Fran the same thing Sheldon wanted to know. Or I could fall back on the truth and tell Sheldon I guessed what was going on between Nicki and Fran. No, I'd never do that. But I'd told myself I wouldn't let Fran kiss me and here I was in my short dress and my slingbacks (black kidskin, two-inch heels) and my red nails and my lips brushed red too. I looked too elegant for the Springer show, or was I kidding myself?

I'll try to tell the truth, I said. That I was having sex with Nicki? Fran said. I thought: I'm here because I want to be here with you. Which was an honest thing to admit, as far as it went. But wasn't I thinking, here I am, now you have to decide what you're going to do about me and that way I don't have to decide and that way I don't have to take responsibility and feel terrible if you kiss me, all of which makes me a terrible person in almost everyone's book except a few who shrug and agree with Mr. Porter that now, heaven knows, anything goes. I was giving Fran a glimpse of something more than stocking, at the same time wondering if he had ever heard of Cole Porter.

There were lots of other issues I wasn't facing either as I swung my leg back and forth and felt the late-August sun on my skin. I closed my eyes and tilted my head. The perfect moment for Fran to kiss me. But he never did.

For supper I cooked Kentucky Wonders and fresh corn to go with chicken. Sheldon and I ate our supper listening to the music on National Public Radio. Let's face the music and dance. Was that a Porter lyric? I couldn't remember. I was ready to face the music. Quite a surprise seeing you today, Sheldon said. I explained that Mr. Hennesy, we'd heard, had resigned his position at the high school. He had borrowed several books from the library and Anne Haber had sent me to recover them before he left town. He told me he'd resigned, Sheldon said sourly. No more questions.

"Are you going home?" Russell asked.

Russell and Nicki sat on the porch drinking the beers he had taken from the bar. Betty didn't mind. Labor Day was over. The September night was full of the sounds of courting crickets. The lodge would close in a few days.

"I've thought about it. What about you?"

"Florida. Work's easy to find there."

Nicki smiled. "And guys?"

"You didn't think you converted me, did you?"

"I thought a couple of times you enjoyed yourself."

Russell put his arms around Nicki. "I did," he said.

"Christmas," Nicki said. "I'll go home then."

"What's in the meantime?"

"Betty's going to recommend me to the Dot & Dash. It's always busy."

"You're overqualified."

"Don't be a snob."

"Maybe you'll meet a sweet trucker and never go home."

"That's your fantasy, not mine," Nicki said.

"Willie like college?" Sheldon asked.

"Willie likes Boston, but I'm not sure how serious he is about school. He went out for fall baseball, but he hurt his hand," Wesley Boots answered.

"How?"

"He wasn't clear on that point, but I guess the injury has something to do with throwing a punch."

"Are you worried?"

"I was a bit wild at his age and not immune to taking a poke at someone who deserved it. But I found my way, and I think Willie will find his."

Wesley paid his tab and left a tip for Jimmy. Sheldon didn't want to go home yet. Harriet was attending a meeting of library staff and volunteers. Sheldon would have another drink and order a steak sandwich at the bar. Jimmy poured Sheldon's Scotch and asked if Sheldon knew a plumber named Henry Blatt. Sheldon shook his head.

"Henry told me his son disappeared in June," Jimmy said. "I doubt he knows about your daughter."

"Must be the only person in town who doesn't."

"Henry sticks to himself. Most of the work he gets is out of town. He doesn't listen very well anyway."

"Would he talk to me?"

"Take him a bottle of rum. He prefers Myers dark."

The library meeting ended around eight. Harriet stood beside Anne Haber in the parking lot. Toothy pumpkin faces glowed in each library window.

"Hungry?" Anne asked.

"I was going to skip dinner," Harriet said.

"Trade you a ride home for a glass of wine."

Anne Haber lived in one of the large old houses on Main Street near the college. She usually walked from her house to the library, even on the bitterest winter days. People referred to her as athletic.

"Last year we had a dusting of snow by now," Anne said.

"Two seasons, winter and getting ready for winter," Harriet said.

"We've known each other twenty years and we still make jokes about New Hampshire weather. What does that tell us?" Anne asked.

"I'm not sure," Harriet said. She stopped the car in front of Anne's house.

"My neighbors think they have it figured out," Anne said. "Straight company parks here. Anyone else leaves her car around the side by the basement door."

"I can move mine if you want to confuse them."

"Or start a rumor. Everyone knows everyone else's car."

Harriet followed Anne up the walk. Geraniums still flourished in pots by the front door. Anne broke off a stem.

"I adore the scent," she said and held out her fingers for Harriet to smell.

Anne turned on some lights. The house was full of antiques. Anne's parents had been collectors.

The kitchen surfaces were white, except for the black countertops and covers on the burners on the stove and the Italian bistro chairs around the table by the long window above the backyard. There were pots of basil, thyme, and chives on the window ledge, among pieces of Anne's Staffordshire. Anne put out some cheese and crackers.

"Heard from Nicki again?"

"She's coming home at Christmas."

"You must be relieved."

"She's not going to be the same Nicki. Any advice?"

"Tell her how you feel."

"That's not usually how I work."

"Me neither, but that's what the mental health gurus tell us to do."

"I haven't told Sheldon yet."

The wine's flavors mixed in subtle, pleasing ways with the Gouda and the Vermont Cheddar. Anne got up for more crackers. Her black sweater and slacks, her skin so white and so smooth Harriet thought Anne looked younger than she did, although Anne was older by five years. A tall woman, almost six feet, too tall to have become the dancer she wanted to be. She'd earned a library degree at Simmons.

"When I came back to Jeffrey, I lived in a tiny house behind the post office. My father suggested it."

"You think Nicki should live on her own?"

"Give yourselves a few months to find out if Nicki needs to."

Anne filled their glasses again. Harriet picked a leaf of basil and bit off the tip, letting the flavor fill up her mouth, aware of Anne watching intently over the rim of her glass.

"So, should the library budget more for audiovisual?" Harriet asked.

"Sorry, I didn't mean to make you nervous," Anne said.

Harriet didn't feel herself blushing. "You didn't."

"Of course I did. I was staring at you."

"I stared at you a minute ago."

"Any thoughts?"

"You have remarkable skin."

"Are you interested?"

"Yes. What's your secret?"

"That's not my question."

Harriet felt the heat on her skin now.

"I lied. I do believe in telling people how I feel. It makes it easier to know how they feel. So I ask," Anne said.

"No one ever asked what I think you're asking."

Anne leaned back and sipped her wine. "I've thought about you a lot, and I'm tired of wondering. I guess you've answered my question. To answer yours, yes, we should budget more for audiovisual."

"You're not angry, are you?"

"Of course not. I didn't invite you here for anything more than talk and wine. I hope you're not angry with me."

"Just puzzled," Harriet said, and squeezed Anne's hand.

III

Willie, be careful.

That was what the voice said. Her voice, Nicki's voice.

Willie heard the voice in bed, his face near the wall. Inside it, ancient duct work shuddered and groaned, then went quiet. Nicki spoke sweetly and clearly into the stillness: Willie, be careful.

Willie tried to embody Nicki's voice into one of the images of Nicki he remembered: Nicki in her hiking shorts; Nicki in tights and a shirt with thin straps; Nicki disarrayed on the boat. But those didn't work. In fact Willie couldn't get Nicki to appear at all. Mist covered her, clung to her, obscured her. Out of mist she spoke: Willie, be careful; and spoke again, Willie, be careful; and again, Willie, be careful.

One night, when the voice roused Willie from sleep, he rose on his knees, cocked his arm, and swung his fist into the wall.

How'd you do that? his teammates asked when they saw his plastered hand with a bit of metal splint poking out the open end. He'd punched a wall, he said, and let them infer from his minimal response that he must have been drunk. At the rush parties someone always called for a round of Willie Wallbangers and everyone laughed. Drinking was easier than studying. But drinking didn't shut out Nicki's voice. Willie, be careful. Willie, be careful.

Everything in its place and I'll be all right, he thought. No matter how hung over he was, each morning Willie made his bed, pulling the sheets and blanket tight and smooth, centering the pillow. He straightened the clothes in his closet. Made sure the creases in his trousers were even, his shoes toe to toe, heel to heel. He hung and rehung his towel, lined up his comb and brush as neatly as he arranged his knife and fork on his cafeteria tray. He walked the same paths to his classes. Sat in the same seats. Retraced his steps at the end of each day. Waited in his room until someone knocked and said time to party.

Sheldon had talked to Mr. Blatt. Afterward Sheldon walked to the lake, along a weedy car path. Nothing between them, nothing romantic, nothing sexual. My son's not the kind, Mr. Blatt said, a man who had no interest in ever seeing his son again. Nothing more to be found out, as far as Sheldon was concerned. Nicki had gotten it into her head to go away. She wasn't the sort of girl she pretended to be. Princeton and all the other opportunities Sheldon had given her didn't matter to her. Saved me money, Sheldon said, and drove back to Jeffrey. He was fond now of settling himself at the bar and drinking a couple of single malts before going home. Harriet was spending more and more time at the library. Tonight someone was speaking, or giving a reading. Harriet was in charge of the series. She'd be late again.

We were standing in Anne's kitchen. I said, Please kiss me. Anne touched my cheek. You sure? she asked. I want to try, I said, which didn't sound quite the note I wanted. All day "All of You" had been running through my mind, especially the line "I'd like to make a tour of you." I really wasn't ready for a tour yet, but I wasn't ready to deny my curiosity either. Don't make a big deal out of this, I told myself. Be as elegant as the lyric. We kissed. I was nervous. Anne was tender.

Our speaker was waiting for us at the inn to escort him to the library. Sheldon was leaving as we arrived. He looked at Anne and his face took on that same puzzled expression I'd seen when we passed each other on Fran's road.

The speaker discussed painters of the Connecticut River Valley. I imagined Thomas Dewing painting me and

Anne. We wear white dresses and attend to picking flowers. The sky is blue, the sun warm. Later Anne and I will go into the house, remove our clothes, and bathe together. "The east of you, the north of you . . ."

I put my hand over my mouth and giggled. I apologized to the speaker at the coffee and dessert table afterward. What were you thinking about? Anne asked. We were parked in front of her house. You and me, I said. Anne leaned over to kiss me goodnight, nothing more than a brush of lips on my cheek, but I turned my mouth toward hers. ". . . complete control of you . . ."

When Nicki comes homes, what do you want me to do? Sheldon asked. Don't expect anything from her, I said. No apologies, no explanations. Show her love, or at least acceptance. I looked into Sheldon's eyes. He was thinking, What's she going to show us?

Snow was starting to fall when the bus stopped in front of the café to let her off. She wore a secondhand coat with a hood on it. She carried a stiff tote bag with a picture of lakes and mountains on one side and Laurel Lodge on the other. I put my arms around her. She had lost weight. So had I.

The voices of the children's choir fill the church. Kneeling, we confess our sins, against God, against our neighbors, things done and left undone. I confess I am falling in love. I confess I don't know what to do. I confess I'm selfish. I confess I don't like growing old. I confess I'm vain and foolish. I confess I'm a terrible parent. I want the holiday to end. The stores to open. The mail to arrive. I need routines, schedules, the hours at the library, Anne close to me.

Does Nicki need me? Hard to tell. She acts like a perfect guest, willing to help or stay out of the way. She reads, listens to music, takes long walks. Once we walk together, up Main Street, the boughs of the spruces heavy with snow. We don't talk. I take her arm. She lets me. I lean against her. She lets me. I am the one who needs comforting. I stop and press my face against hers. I am the one who cries. I tell her how sorry I am. We continue down the street, our breath disappearing in the gray air.

The library reopens. By the time I come home, Nicki has shopped and prepared supper. Sheldon tastes and approves.

New Year's Eve. The Bootes always have a party. Willie's in town, more or less permanently, according to Sheldon. See you there, Nicki says. Sheldon is looking pleased: What? I ask. Nicki tells me Vi Willis is catering the party and asked Nicki to help.

The Bootes have a hot tub. Sheldon reminds me to bring a bathing suit. I borrow Nicki's tote bag and stuff my suit inside, along with Sheldon's and a couple of bottles of wine.

A clear, cold night. Couples crowd the deck to watch the northern lights. Through the window I see Nicki in a skirt and blouse passing trays, this one covered with skewered lamb. I used to call her that, my lamb. My lovely lamb. She stands tall and is patient with the guests, who dip the lamb into spicy mint sauce that drips on their clothes. She balances the tray and hands out napkins. Does she notice people whispering about her? Does she care?

Then I see Willie, just passing through, shaking a few hands on his way to the door where Mike is waiting. Willie sees Nicki. He goes absolutely motionless, frozen, his hand in the flabby grip of Hilton Woolrich. Nicki approaches and offers what's on her tray. Spring rolls this time. Willie springs, bolts for the door, pulling Hilton with him before he can let go. Mike and Willie disappear. No change in Nicki's professional smile. No clue what she's thinking. She kneels to wipe up the wine Hilton spilled.

At midnight I find Nicki and hug her. We have the deck to ourselves. I keep my arm around her. We pass champagne back and forth until the glass is empty.

I tell Sheldon I'm not in the mood for the hot tub. He goes by himself. I put on my coat and walk toward the lake and call Anne on my cell phone. She's in bed reading the book I gave her for Christmas. We wish each other a happy New Year.

After the holidays, sometimes Harriet saw Willie driving a company truck. Delivering samples of floor covering, ceiling tiles, and hardware to subcontractors, Sheldon said. Willie refused to use the interstate. Too much black ice. He preferred back roads. Willie, be careful. Willie, be careful.

Nicki enrolled in classes at Shippen. In the afternoons, when Harriet was working at the library, Nicki shopped. If Harriet was late, Nicki cooked. She took clothes to the dry cleaner every Monday. Every Friday, she picked them up. If Willie saw her walking to the college, he pulled over and waited until she was out of sight. He always peered through shop windows to make sure Nicki wasn't anywhere he was going. He bought seven pairs of identical socks, three of the same sweatshirts, and three pairs of green corduroys. It calmed him to dress the same every day. You dress like an old man, Mike said.

Mike worked in an auto parts store in Newport. He met a girl whose father had a snowmobile and let them run it over the lake. Willie joined them sometimes. Mike's girl offered to invite another girl for Willie, but he told her not to. Willie liked to walk on the lake by himself. No one around, everything in place. Everything clean and bright. No voices. Only the wind. He gave one of the men who worked for his father money to buy him some vodka. Willie walked up and down the lake, the vodka pure and warm fueling his body.

Nicki made new friends. One Saturday she drove with them to Hanover for an exhibition of paintings at the Hood. She saw her mother and Anne Haber eating lunch together. They didn't notice Nicki. Her mother whispered something in Anne's ear.

One painter in the show Nicki had never heard of, Thomas Dewing. He painted women in white dresses walking in summer gardens. The light was lovely on the flowers and on their skin. Nicki remembered the way the light slanted through the restaurant window and shined on the nape of her mother's neck and the brow of Anne Haber.

One night in March, just before the weather changed, then changed again, Sheldon was in New York. Nicki had stayed late at the college. There was a dance. She was walking across the campus and saw me coming out of Anne's house. Nearly midnight. I was walking too because for a week the weather had been so warm. We walked home together. Nicki said she'd had a good time at the dance. She asked me if I had a good time, the hesitation in her voice indicating she would leave it up to me to say what I might have had a good time doing. Anne cooked supper and I stayed late drinking wine, I said. In a kind voice, not accusatory at all, Nicki said, You don't smell like wine, you smell like Anne Haber. Nicki sounded motherly, as if she'd known all the time about Anne and me and wanted me to know she knew and wouldn't give advice or interfere. Nicki had one of those amused smiles mothers smile when they see their children becoming adults. We were almost home when the rain started. I can't remember such a warm rain in March.

So still, so perfect, Willie thought, the warm air, the fog rising off the ice. So incredibly warm. Then the rain. He put down the bottle, careful not to spill any of the vodka, and raised his arms to the sky. His fingertips felt it, the nip of different air, the chill concealed in the tepid fog. He was always good about predicting weather. Before morning the wind would be north.

He picked up the bottle and continued to walk. So perfect. No one could find him here, no voices. When he heard the sound, he didn't pay much attention. Ice made sounds. When he slipped, he didn't pay much attention. He slipped a lot on ice. Then he understood and he lay down and stretched out and tried to crawl in the direction he thought was shore. The ice sagged, broke apart. He lunged to pull himself forward. He was wet now. The water was heavy. It filled his clothes. He called into the fog for help. His voice came back to him, each time farther and farther away.

By dawn several inches of fresh snow. The temperature fell all morning. For days it stayed at zero. Sheldon returned from New York. I first heard at the market that Willie was missing. Of course people thought of the lake. If he left any tracks, though, the snow covered them. Wesley remained hopeful. He said, Willie had become strange. He might have gone off somewhere, like Nicki. I asked her what she thought. She was wearing one of my old aprons and serving breakfast. Sheldon was particularly fond of her pancakes. She said she didn't think about Willie at all. She reminded Sheldon about some notes he was to take to a meeting with a new client.

In April the weather turned to spring. Orange poles went up to warn people to stay off the ice. Soon boats began to appear on the lake again. Haywood Burns towed his seaplane to its mooring. Willie's clothes had caught on it. Some troopers brought the body back to shore.

The church service was private. There was a wake to celebrate Willie's life. Willie's mother wanted to do the food herself, but Nicki fixed most of it. She stayed to clean up. Wesley said to Sheldon, You have a remarkable daughter. Sheldon said, I think so too.

On the way home I drowsed in the backseat. I heard Sheldon and Nicki talking, their voices chatty, friendly. Their words sounded close by and comforting. But when I tried to understand what the words meant, they became obscure and remote. They had nothing to do with me.

～ CAR TALK ～

Arlene Givens does it more and more now, drives by the house on Dutchman's Hill where Vi Willis lives, a small house, only one bedroom, but adequate for Vi and her cat. The remodeled kitchen suits Vi too. She's in the catering business. She's never asked her former husband, an accountant, for alimony.

Even when Dutchman's Hill is out of her way, Arlene drives by the house. On these warm evenings, Arlene often sees Vi sitting in the yard in moonlight stroking the cat on her lap. A bomber's moon, Arlene remembers Lew saying.

Piet DeMonye was the Dutchman. In the nineteenth century the hill had been his farm. Sheep and cows and goats and stone walls. Now the tumbled stones separate small parcels of land. During World War II, the students from the college trained as plane spotters, taking turns standing on the hill studying the sky, vigilant for the German bombers that might fly a northern route over the Atlantic, then dip south to attack Boston or New York.

Lew's war had been Korea. In 1951 his plane fell into the ocean, his body not recovered, information it took Arlene a year to find out. Lew had been twenty-one, Arlene eighteen, and Vi a month from being born.

Lew had big hands and blue eyes. He smiled sweetly and talked in a southern accent, a bit more country than her own. He'd worked as a mechanic before enlisting. He was crazy about sex and cars.

Arlene had left Virginia at sixteen. She found work at a factory in Claremont, an hour from Jeffrey, but really another world away. Gwen, who was older and had a year at business college and worked in payroll, became Arlene's friend. Gwen was married to Walt Hughes. When the Chinese overran Walt's company, he was killed too.

After the war, Arlene, Gwen, and Vi moved to Jeffrey and lived together in a rented house on a street behind the town green. Arlene worked at the drugstore. Gwen managed a clothing shop. When Edgar Willis, a young dentist in town, proposed, Gwen accepted. An agent named Hadley Lampkin sold Gwen and Edgar an old house with an attached barn that need fixing up. Hadley Lampkin had an affair with Arlene. She confided to Gwen that Hadley's postcoital chat was about the property business. Gradually Arlene became interested in real estate herself. Gwen was interested in decorating. Over time, Gwen changed. Sometimes Arlene felt Gwen's disapproval. Nevertheless, Aunt Arlene was always welcomed at Gwen and Edgar's house. Arlene never forgot Vi's birthdays, always gave Vi a modest gift. We have a wonderful daughter, Gwen said walking Arlene to her car. Vi and her friends were tie-dying their clothes in the kitchen. *We,* to everyone else, would mean Gwen and Edgar. Only Gwen and Arlene knew that Arlene was Vi's mother.

Edgar collected rugs, traveled, and lived beyond his means. Cancer forced him to retire at sixty. Gwen sold the rugs one by one to pay for Edgar's care. Gwen died six months ago, her estate worth fifty thousand dollars. With the money Vi had remodeled the kitchen and bought a new Subaru. Guess I can't afford to be sick or quit working, Vi said.

Arlene had wanted to say, I'm your mother, not Gwen, and I have money and when I die it's all yours. One evening a year ago at the inn, Arlene had come close to letting the words rush out. She had been sitting at her usual table in the corner of the taproom, looking over some contracts. She was finishing her first martini when Vi appeared and took a seat at the bar. Arlene carried her glass to the bar to ask Jimmy for a refill. Meeting someone? she asked. Aunt Arlene, Vi managed to say. Don't be surprised. I'm here almost every evening. Are you meeting someone? Vi shook her head. Then join me, Arlene said.

Vi ordered sparkling water. Jimmy brought Perrier to the table with Arlene's martini. You came in here for that? Arlene asked. She saw Jimmy smile. I'm not much of a drinker, Aunt Arlene, Vi said.

Arlene and Vi ended up ordering supper. Arlene selected a Beaujolais. Vi drank a couple of glasses. Jimmy offered complimentary Kahlúas with their coffee. I don't like to think about money, Vi said. Too depressing. That's when Arlene wanted to reach over and hold Vi's hands and tell her everything. But no. Despite three martinis, wine, and Kahlúa Arlene didn't. Money talk was the wrong place to begin. There was no love in it. They called it a night.

Arlene replayed the night again and again. Why was Vi there? She said she wasn't meeting anyone, and no one showed up looking for her. She's not the type to go to a bar and spend money on the same sparkling water she can drink free at home. Jimmy? Could it be Jimmy? That dark skin, those delicate fingers . . . Arlene has thought one or two things about Jimmy herself. Jimmy's Vi's age. People like him. Half a dozen regulars have long discussions with him. That's about all Arlene knows about Jimmy.

One night, very late, on her way home from a meeting in Hanover, Arlene sees Jimmy's car next to Vi's Subaru. The house lights are off, all except one in the bedroom. She'll bet Jimmy is better than Vi's ex, who preferred, so Gwen implied, balance sheets to bedsheets. Let Vi be happy. Let Jimmy be happy. Let me be happy, Arlene says.

Arlene isn't happy. Arlene isn't happy because she needs to tell Vi how wanted she was. How she was conceived in exquisite passion. Lew, be gentle, Arlene cautioned, already certain the first seconds of Vi's life had begun. Not *Vi*, Amanda Jane was the name Arlene picked out. Vi was Gwen's choice. She had seen *Gone With the Wind* ten times and worshiped Vivian Leigh.

Arlene would start this way: You have to realize we lived differently in the fifties. People believed what you said. I told them at the hospital my name was Gwen Hughes and Walter Hughes was my baby's father.

The next part of the story is funny if you think about it, Arlene would continue. I wanted to see where Lew had grown up, learn more about him. I traveled to Harp, Kentucky: a diner, a grocery, a feed store, a gas station, two churches, and a scattering of houses. Lew was a Ramsey. I wandered through a cemetery looking for Ramseys. I found a couple of them. A man wearing a white suit and a straw hat saw me. His name was Davis. He asked what I was doing. I explained I was engaged once to Lew Ramsey. You won't find him here, Davis said. I said, If the town didn't have a war memorial, I expected the county seat had one and I'd find Lew's name on it. Davis appeared amused. He told me Lew Ramsey lived at Mrs. Pritchard's boardinghouse. If I needed a place to stay that night he said to come back.

Lew Ramsey sat in a wheelchair in his room watching the television on the dresser. I told him I had come from New Hampshire, that I'd been engaged to a flyer whose name, I thought, was Lew Ramsey.

Probably Collier Noles, Mr. Ramsey said. He described perfectly the man I loved, right down to his crooked smile and his fascination with cars. As it turned out, Collier Noles had driven several cars he had no one's permission to drive, a situation that caused the sheriff to encourage him to leave town. Often he had a young lady in his car, Mr. Ramsey said. Sometimes more than one. He had his way with them. He was a lady's man through and through. I wasn't, Mr. Ramsey said. I was all churchy about how I treated women. Collier would think it funny to use my name. Ironic, I suppose you'd say. I hope you didn't count on him being faithful and returning to you.

Arlene hears herself telling Vi all those things. Vi is looking at Arlene in disbelief. Arlene is making everything up. Gwen was my mother. Walter Hughes was my father. He died. Edgar Willis adopted me. Not one scrap of paper says anything about Arlene Givens and Lew Ramsey.

Gwen was a good mother. A good friend. Arlene is ashamed that she wants to tell Vi that Gwen wasn't her mother. What have I got to take credit for? Arlene asks herself. One more girl who believed her lover was going to marry her. The only thing special about my situation was thinking I knew my lover's name and I didn't know his name at all.

Arlene stops driving by Vi's house. Arlene gives up her usual corner table and chooses a seat at the end of the bar. She arrives after seven. Rudy and the other regulars have gone home. She and Jimmy talk. They are outsiders, both from somewhere else. Most of the town is from somewhere else. The old families have died off. But the newcomers are really insiders. They've gone to summer camps on the lake, or they've learned to ski on Mount Blue, or they've attended the same colleges. They've lived in cities in Massachusetts and New York and Connecticut and made money and come to Jeffrey to retire.

People leave you alone here, Jimmy says. He owns part of the inn now. He has plans to improve it.

Leave you alone completely? Never any raised eyebrows? Never a door that isn't gladly open to you? Arlene asks.

I wouldn't want to live anywhere all the doors were gladly open to me, Jimmy says.

I've made so many people angry, doors are shut in my face all the time, Arlene says. Jimmy goes away to mix some drinks for the crowd in the dining room.

You know, Jimmy says when he comes back, you and Vi look a lot alike.

Same color eyes, maybe.

More than that, Jimmy says. Same mouth, same nose.

Same gene pool, Arlene replies.

Probably, Jimmy says. Christie from the dining room asks Jimmy for two more stingers.

How long have you and Vi been seeing each other? Arlene asks. The question doesn't surprise Jimmy.

A couple of months.

Any plans?

My God, do I want grandchildren? Arlene wonders.

We're doing okay without plans right now, Jimmy says.

Arlene finishes her drink, pays her tab, and wishes Jimmy goodnight.

She drives home. Well, one more detour won't matter: There wasn't any place to stay. Davis invited me to sleep at his house. We sat in the kitchen drinking Wild Turkey and talking. Davis asked if I had a snapshot of you. I didn't. There used to be photographs. Every birthday party. Vi and Aunt Arlene.

Arlene tries to remember when Gwen stopped taking photographs. Arlene and Vi in the same picture was a bad idea. Vi could compare their faces in a way she never could without the faces being in front of her. Before the similarities became too obvious, Gwen had stopped taking pictures.

The next day Arlene closes on a house before noon and has a contract lined up on another by five o'clock. At six she's sitting at her corner table again. Rudy and some of the other regulars are leaning on the bar joking with Jimmy. When Jimmy brings her drink, they talk about the weather. They don't mention Vi at all.

Once more. One last time, Arlene promises herself.

Tonight it's raining. Vi won't be sitting in the yard. Arlene parks up the street, in the driveway of a rundown Saltbox that's been on the market for months. She opens the car window and smells the scent of pines in the wet August air. Davis's house was a Victorian with steep stairs. Davis had a bad leg and slept in a room on the first floor. I went upstairs and bathed in a tub with claw feet. I dried myself and climbed into a soft bed. When I woke, I wasn't afraid. I recognized the face. I knew his name now. Collier, I said. He smiled. He was sitting beside my bed. He leaned over and put his hand on where you were inside me, then laid his head on my skin as if he could hear you breathe. After a while he pushed back the chair. He kissed his fingers and touched you. Then he was by the door. Then the room was empty. He loves you and I love you.

Arlene sits in her car listening to the rain. That's what I want to tell you, she says.

~ YES ~

Elizabeth Lodge is eating Sunday brunch at the inn with her friends Ruthie and Doris. Doris compliments the monkfish. Reminds me of lobster, she says. Elizabeth glances up from her fruit platter. Beyond Doris's left ear, near the bar entrance, Elizabeth sees Wayne, her husband, a sturdy man whose favorite meal is Sunday supper, always served an hour after coming home from church, and always preceded by a cocktail. Wayne stands between two windows and looks in Elizabeth's direction. The light is confusing, but she's sure it's Wayne. She raises her arm as if to wave, but instead reaches out with trembling fingers for Doris's wrist. Wayne has been dead for five years.

Boyd Wagner lives in a building behind the bank. The building has windows and green shutters to make it appear something other than it is, a cinder-block rectangle the county used as a storage garage until 1950. Ten years later, Boyd's father, who owned the property by then, added a mansard roof with cedar shingles. He intended to divide the building into retail spaces, six businesses in all, but the Colonial Wash & Dry was the only one to show interest, so he rented the building to a bulk mailing company, which moved to larger quarters in 1995, a year before Boyd's father died. Wooden steps in the back of the building lead to Boyd's apartment, formerly the offices of the three employees who ran the mail business. Below, the entire floor space, five thousand square feet, once filled by forklifts and pallets of catalogs, is occupied by a single car, a yellow 1946 Ford convertible. On Sunday afternoons Boyd opens the wide overhead doors. Passersby on Main Street can look in and see the car, and Boyd sitting on a chair in the sunshine reading a copy of *Hemmings Motor News,* perusing the advertisements for parts.

Trish Griswold opens the bookstore on Sundays. Nancy, her business partner, opens the store Saturdays. Trish is alone until one, when Lisa, recently returned from her honeymoon, arrives to open boxes, enter new books into the computer, and dust.

Cool, you ordered a copy, Lisa exclaims, holding up *O, Oh Yes,* a how-to for achieving female orgasm written by Susan Simoné, the other woman to a series of lovers on daytime television. Against her better judgment, Trish did order a copy. Her customers are mostly late sixties, early seventies. The women buy best-sellers, gardening books, and travel guides (Tuscany is always popular); the men, military histories, fishing books, and sea stories (*yarns,* they call them). Copies of the *Joy Of Sex* never sold. Will this book be any different? Maybe a tourist will be interested, but Trish isn't going to feature *O, Oh Yes* on the front tables with the other new titles.

Liz, are you all right, dear? Ruthie asks. Not that pain again?

Elizabeth is too embarrassed to tell what she saw. I'm fine, she says. I am.

After dividing the check, Elizabeth drives to the Knolls. Ruthie and Doris have accommodations in the assisted living section. Elizabeth lives in the apartments where residents cook their own meals and take care of themselves. Actually, her health is more fragile than her friends', though Elizabeth hasn't told them. Now we can only hope to control your pain, the doctor said. Elizabeth used to think her faith would get her through it, the dying. She's not so certain anymore. She swallows one of the pills her doctor prescribed for pain and lies down. Wayne, you're here, aren't you? she says. I saw you, didn't I? I really did.

Her eyes closed, Elizabeth holds out her hand awaiting Wayne's touch. She circles her arm back and forth in the empty air. She feels only a draft from the window. Almost time to close the storms.

At three o'clock a few cars, most towing boats, go up and down Main Street. Boyd pulls down the doors, jams his dirty clothes into his backpack, and walks to the Wash & Dry at its new location in the shopping center.

Boyd fills the washer and sets the timer. He's alone

except for a woman whose clothes are tumbling in the dryer. She leans on one of the washers talking on her phone. I asked you to, but you didn't do it, she says. I guess I'm not important.

Boyd dislikes cell phones. He asked a tourist at the café across from the green to put his away. Boyd is six feet tall. He used to lift weights and has a fading tattoo from his time in Vietnam. The man tucked his phone into his pocket.

The woman is wearing a white shirt decorated with orange beadwork, jeans, and boots with pointed toes. Not from around here, as the locals say. Boyd noticed the Tennessee plate on the Toyota pickup parked by the door. The woman says, You know that's a lie, and snaps her phone shut.

The dryer turns off. The woman scoops her clothes into a plastic basket. She balances the basket against her hip and regards Boyd. Where can I get a beer? she asks.

The Cove on Main Street. Boyd points out the window. They have good sandwiches too. Or the inn. The bar opens at five on Sunday.

Boyd notices the package of cigarettes in the woman's shirt pocket. Can't smoke at either one, he says.

Figures, the woman says. She pauses at the door and glances back at Boyd. Sorry. I'm not usually so rude. I appreciate your answering my question.

Lisa has spent her free time sitting on a stool, feather duster in one hand, the other turning the pages of *O*,

Oh Yes. Trish is tempted to ask how the honeymoon went, but decides against it. There's some neat stuff in here, Lisa says. You mean "good advice"? Lisa's casual speech dismays Trish. Lisa isn't ready for customers yet.

Stuff about my body even I didn't know, Lisa says. Maybe Lisa will buy the copy. Trish reminds Lisa about the employee discount, but she doesn't make the connection.

I'll shelve it in Health, Lisa says. What about Self-Help? Trish asks. I put *Sex for One* there. This you need a man for, Lisa answers. A *partner* you mean, Trish corrects her. Whatever, Lisa says. Another entry in Lisa's vocabulary that annoys Trish. She dismisses the idea of ordering a second copy to add to the tiny Gay and Lesbian section, to the left of Personal Finance.

Monday morning. Boyd walks down Main Street to the college where he works part time in the library. The students are gone in the summer. A research conference is taking place, lots of men with beards and white legs. Lots of cell phones.

Boyd is fifty-two. Other than two years at Harvard and two years in Vietnam, he's always lived in Jeffrey. He doesn't need to work, but he thinks he should. Today he's checking the shelf list, finding what's missing, putting books in their proper order. The student shelvers are careless. Boyd isn't. This morning it's the TRs, photography. Most of the volumes are large and heavy. They lean. Boyd straightens them. He sits on the tiny stool in the middle of an aisle under a fluorescent light balancing a collection of Imogen Cunningham on his knees. The nudes are geometric, chaste. Sometimes he'll remember a girl he kissed at a party in Cambridge, sometimes a woman he slept with in Vietnam. Usually he doesn't think of women at all, but now he remembers the woman with her laundry basket and the smells of her sweat, perfume, and cigarettes.

Elizabeth is sitting in the bright air on a bench on the green. She watches people leaving the church, a service for Tommy Wharton. She should have attended, but her mind is so much on her own death that she can't sit through someone else's service. Then, gazing through the shafts of light, she sees Wayne appear at the church door. He's dressed in the gray suit he bought at J. Press years ago during a Harvard reunion, the suit he always wears to funerals. He looks her way. Surely he sees her. He pauses. Then he disappears. Please, Wayne, please. I need you, she says. She stops herself and glances around to see if anyone nearby is listening.

You sold it, Lisa exclaims, beginning her afternoon unpacking of the UPS delivery.

It?

O, Oh Yes.

I didn't. I'll ask Nancy if she did.

Not me. I would remember, Nancy says when she returns from lunch.

Trish checks the shelves, no book. Damned if she'll order another. Nancy whispers to Trish that Lisa seems rather smiley and dreamy today.

Around four o'clock the shop is quiet. Nancy is doing inventory. Lisa, wearing headphones, is off in her own world. Philip comes to bother Trish. A handsome man, quite a catch, Trish's mother said. A doctor too. Trish's mother would have stayed married to a man like Philip. The parties, the income, the social standing, put those on one side and the man's ego and his objection to certain acts of intimacy (how prudish he was about the female body) on the other, and the negatives would have no weight at all the way Trish's mother read the scale. But the balance was all wrong to Trish. Trish's daughter, who lives in Denver, is the only good thing from the marriage. Philip has remarried. Trish has not.

~

Tuesday. Boyd usually eats lunch at the café but he decides she wouldn't, the woman from the Wash & Dry. The Cove is more her style, rustic, no frills, country music in the background. She's probably left town, but Boyd stands in the dim light scanning the tables. She's drinking at the bar. He pretends not to see her, slides into a booth, opens his newspaper. He's finished most of his three-bean salad when she leans over his shoulder.

Eating healthy?

Trying to, Boyd answers.

The woman sits down beside him. I'm drinking healthy, she says, holding up her bottle. Light beer and only two.

On vacation? Boyd asks.

More like on the run. From love or something like it. She closes her eyes and repeats "from love or something like it," singing the words softly. Sounds like a song, she says, but I can't find a second line.

You write songs? Boyd asks.

I've done a few.

Would I know any?

You listen to country music?

No.

Then you wouldn't. I haven't had any crossover hits yet. Of course I haven't had any hits of any kind.

Her phone rings. She fishes it from her jeans pocket and goes outside, listening on the way, Boyd watching her swaying hips.

You can run but you can't hide, she says when she sits down again.

Not if you carry a phone.

You don't have one?

No.

Well, I told him not to call me anymore. Ever. Now, where were we?

You were about to order lunch, Boyd says.

And another beer, she says.

Today several customers have come in expecting Trish to tell them what book they want to read, as if she were an oracle or a therapist. The phone call is a welcome distraction. The voice says, So, this vulture gets on a plane to Seattle. The vulture has a dead racoon in each claw. The flight attendant bustles down the aisle and tells the vulture he can't have both raccoons. Why? the vulture asks. Because it's company policy, only one carrion per passenger.

I thought the vulture was flying to Atlanta, Trish says to her daughter.

Love you, Mom.

Love you too, Sweetie.

Wednesday. Elizabeth wakes up. From her place in bed she thinks she can see the window at the end of the hall outside her bedroom door. She is sure a figure has just passed along the hall and vanished into the east light blurring the panes of glass. She is sure it was Wayne. Around her she can feel his presence lingering like warmth in a room after the sun changes places.

But she can't see what she thinks she sees. The hall isn't there. The window isn't there. They were there in the house where she and Wayne lived. The small apartments in the Knolls have no such space or architecture.

Elizabeth puts on her robe, makes coffee, drinks it, remembering how her dying mother believed Elizabeth's face at her bedside was her own father's, Elizabeth's grandfather, and carried on tender conversations with him. Maybe we all die in the past, Wayne commented when she told him about it. No, the pain is right here in the present. Elizabeth scarcely thinks of anything else except pain and what's going to happen.

Around eleven, several customers are browsing the new titles. A couple of the older regulars from the Knolls have bought things. Maddy Filmore, a favorite of Trish, who always carries her own canvas shopping bag and never accepts bags from stores, purchased some paperbacks for herself and a Bach CD for her Glenn, her husband. So far, a good morning.

On her way to the coffee station, Trish notices the place where *O, Oh Yes* wasn't yesterday. It's there today. *O, Oh Yes* has returned. She lifts it from the shelf. The cover, black background with a huge, pink O, is fresh and new, but the binding is looser. Someone besides Lisa has been turning the pages.

Usually Trish has a good eye for shoplifters, although not the will to confront them outside the store, a legal requirement to charge someone. If the same person tries it twice, she will say loudly, Are you buying that or moving it? Now Trish is trying to imagine who brought back the book. Maddy's bag would make it easy. Maddy though? She and Glenn are seventy-five.

The woman's name is Donnie Stanton. At the start of the hike she explained to Boyd that her father only wanted boys, so he gave her a boy's name. She changed the spelling.

The hike was Donnie's idea. She saw a map of trails at the information hut near the bank. Time to stop moping and move this old body.

The body in question doesn't look old to Boyd, perhaps a couple of years younger than his own. Donnie is as tall as Boyd, but slender. She has brown eyes, long fingers, and skin used to being outside in strong sun. They've been hiking an hour. They sit on a boulder beside a stream rushing over shiny black rocks.

Donnie kicks off her boots. Her jeans are too tapered to roll up, so she unhooks her belt and pulls them off. Her shirt covers the tops of her legs. She walks into the water and stands there, hands raised to the sky. Boyd can see the muscles in her legs flex. He suddenly wants Donnie to put her arms around him and press her shirt to his mouth.

Closing up, Trish takes a last look around. Her eyes drift down the titles in the Health section. Gone again.

No *Oh Yes*. She posts a store best-seller list by the counter. Why not a best-disappearer list too?

∽

Thursday. Elizabeth's doctor stops for coffee at the café. Elizabeth is taking her morning walk, slower each day. Tell me about the pain, he says. The pills control it, she says, but I always know it's there. The doctor smiles and backs into his Cherokee, careful not to spill his coffee on his pressed chinos.

Boyd sits staring at the books. After the hike, he and Donnie had eaten supper together and he showed her the Ford, the car his father bought when he returned from the service, parked twenty years in a damp garage. When she asked for a ride, Boyd explained he wouldn't drive the car until he'd finished restoring it completely. All he needed to do was install a new motor for the top. The old one was broken and the top wouldn't go up anymore.

So you don't own another car and you walk everywhere? Donnie asked.

Boyd nodded.

A Yankee eccentric.

I think I'm normal, Boyd said.

When she kissed him, he felt normal.

On his way to meet Donnie for lunch, Boyd remembers his father telling him, When love calls you,

you don't have to answer. That advice from a man who returned to France in 1947 to find the woman who'd run toward his tank with wine and kisses, Boyd's mother, who lives in Oregon now.

Bought you something, Donnie says, handing Boyd a box from Radio Shack. Now you have your own phone, in case I need to call you.

It's back, Lisa says.

O, Oh Yes has returned, its cover smudged now, especially the lowercase *yes* that flows across the edge of the huge *O,* and the binding looser than ever. How many people have read this book? And who are they? Trish recalls Flo Bordman coming in earlier wearing a raincoat. Except for the odd man who walks past the store every day with an umbrella, Flo seems to be the only person expecting rain. She could certainly conceal a book under the coat. Flo? She's seventy.

Late in the day, Nancy takes over while Trish drives to the post office and the bank. On her way back into the store carrying the mail, Trish glances at Health.

Lisa and Trish stare at the empty space. Lisa says, Think of all the good we're doing. Trish has no comment.

∼

Friday. The PNs are all mixed up. But my life isn't, Boyd thinks. Donnie drinks too much and smokes too much. A few more days, she'll leave town, he'll forget her.

Elizabeth has fixed herself a cup of tea. She sits in the kitchen staring out the window. Wayne, why aren't you here? she asks.

I am here, the voice answers.

She doesn't dare turn around. She keeps staring out the window at the maple tree.

You'll be all right, Liz. You have the pills.

Tell me what happens.

You're here and then you're not.

Where *will* I be?

With me.

But I'm with you now.

Not the way I'm thinking of.

I don't understand.

One moment you're in your body, the next moment you're not. Except there are no more moments. You'll be on the other side of them.

I'm scared, Wayne.

You're scared thinking about it.

I don't like the waiting.

It won't be long, Liz. You won't be alone. I'll be with you. I promise.

Elizabeth keeps looking out the window. A sheen of light covers the maple. Wind tosses the leaves up and down, turning them dark with bright edges.

A late rush of customers wanting books for the weekend, mostly mysteries. Archer Mayor is a favorite since he writes about Vermont, which makes him more or less local.

Of course the local mystery is *O, Oh Yes,* which reappeared on Nancy's watch around the middle of the day. She can't remember who was in the store then. Now the book's too worn to sell at full price.

One by one the customers depart. Nancy and Lisa have gone home. The store should be closed by now, but Eileen Thomas is still perusing the children's section for a gift for her granddaughter. Take your time, Trish says and steps into the bathroom. Eileen and her husband, Fletcher, attend the same church Trish goes to. Eileen and Fletcher have been married forever. Two feisty senior citizens who put on their skis when the lake freezes over and glide across it, then go home and drink martinis in front of a roaring fire.

Trish opens the door. Eileen is on her knees in the Health section shoving *O, Oh Yes* into her tote bag. Trish pulls the door almost closed and watches. Slowly Eileen stands up. Trish gives Eileen enough time to walk to the counter.

Find anything?

Yes, Eileen says. My granddaughter's read all the *Potter* books, so I got this one. Trish types the title into the computer. The price prints on the screen. Gift wrap? Trish asks. No thanks. Fletch is waiting in the car. He gets impatient. Eileen starts to leave. On second thought, wrap the book. I'll pick it up tomorrow.

We're open Sunday, you know.

Sunday would be better. Not so much rush. See you Sunday.

See you, Trish says.

Trish locks the door behind Eileen and turns off the lights. Trish parks her car in the lot behind the store. The wind surprises her. Two people in the next car are kissing, Lisa and her husband, Ken. Lisa left thirty minutes ago. Have they been out here kissing since then? More power to them. Lisa frees an arm and waves, but the kissing doesn't stop. Driving home, Trish turns on the radio, hears the high wind alert. Gusts up to seventy miles an hour by midnight. And rain.

∼

Wind whines. Rain lashes the windows. At first Boyd doesn't hear his phone beeping. He has to search for it.

The wind blew me off the road, Donnie says.

She's crying. She doesn't know where she is. She describes the road. He sees her truck against huge trees, windshield smashed, gobs of mud and weeds stuck in the wheels and bumpers.

Rain beats sideways. The vacuum wipers can't clear the sheeting water. Boyd hunches forward. Water pours down his neck. The headlights barely shine a car's length ahead. Branches fly through the air battering the fenders. Nevertheless, the car speeds forward.

Trish feels as if a hand is shaking her house. Better to be outside. She stands in her driveway, wind whipping the hem of her robe, water running down her face. The wind is striking the steeple bells causing them to ring. Giddy, Trish feels her heels lift off the ground, feels her body borne up to the steeple. All the townspeople are gathered below. Lisa and Flo are there, and Lisa's husband, and that man with the old car, and Maddy and Glenn, and Eileen and Fletcher, and so many others all listening to the bells, listening to the bells ring out for love, love carnal and spiritual, passionate and forgetful, greedy and giving, and all degrees in between. Trish raises her hand in blessing.

Elizabeth hears the bells too. She closes her eyes. The bells are sounding for her funeral. There are the cars nosing into spaces around the church. There is her body in the box that will lie next to the box containing Wayne. But she and Wayne are idling on the green. Wasn't it as I told you it would be? Wayne asks. It was, she says. It was. Yes.

∽ BE YOU ∽

In the trades, Dutch Donovan is described as either rash and heedless or a visionary whose deliberations are measured in nanoseconds. In any case, he makes quick and unexpected choices.

During the eighties Dutch bought lake property. Someone sent him photographs and ten minutes later he bought what he liked. The real estate market was depressed then. He paid $200,000 for a house and frontage worth $2,000,000 now. He would never have heard of Jeffrey, New Hampshire, except for his mother.

The eighties were good to Dutch. His *Wunderkind* years. His play in New York did modest business winning a Tony and an Obie. His films did huge business and won four Oscars. The nineties were all right, profits still there, but critical acclaim declined. Dutch began to spend more time each summer at his house on the lake. He brings a different woman every year, always someone who wears a baseball cap to shade her eyes and keep people from noticing her. Always blondes, always slim, always younger than Dutch by twenty years.

Dutch still has the copy of *Life* magazine with his mother's picture in it. She sits at a table, her hands folded in prayer. A roasted bird on a platter and serving dishes of potatoes, squash, and Brussels sprouts are close by. "Her first Thanksgiving" the caption says. Elena Kupnick is thirteen years old. She looks nine, the age she was when she last ate as much as a single meal a day. She is one of many children sent by relief agencies to Jeffrey between 1944 and 1945. More than a hundred children in all.

After the war, most of the children returned to Europe. Elena stayed in America, living with a cousin in Atlantic City. She never forgot Jeffrey. Dutch bought the house for her, but she was too fragile for her doctors to permit her to leave California, where she lived in another home Dutch had bought for her.

Dutch is back, someone will say. Dutch sightings are what the locals talk about in the summer when they're not discussing the weather. Dutch on his boat on the lake at sunset. Dutch playing golf by himself in the early morning, the course wet with dew. Dutch musing over the selection of ports at the state store. Dutch buying the *Times* on Sunday at the Stop 'n Go. Dutch and his blond companion eating a nine o'clock supper at the inn, usually the only ones in the dining room at that hour. After dinner Dutch and his friend often sit in the bar. Jimmy stocks a couple of the ports Dutch likes.

Lionel Foster knows Dutch better than anyone else in town. Lionel runs the Barn Stage, the summer theater in the building that was once a livery stable.

Lionel chooses the plays and directs most of them. He often asks Dutch for advice.

This year, 2001, is the two hundred and fiftieth anniversary of Jeffrey's founding. A wonderful new history of Jeffrey was published in March. Although Peterborough, New Hampshire, claims to be the model for the fictional town of Grover's Corners in Thornton Wilder's *Our Town*, the history made a reasonable case for Jeffrey. Wilder once worked near Jeffrey and often paused in his walks at Jeffrey's old town graveyard, to which the graveyard in Grover's Corners bears a strong resemblance. There are other similarities, too.

Lionel decided to do a production of *Our Town*, with residents playing all the parts. He wrote Dutch and asked him to choose the players and direct. Dutch agreed.

Dutch arrived, minus a blonde this time, in May. Wreaths of wet snow lay under the trees. The temperature hadn't reached sixty yet. Dutch had to buy a sweater and gloves. A notice for tryouts appeared in the paper. People were already talking about who Dutch should select to play the Stage Manager. Three or four local actors seemed up to the part. Simon DeWitt was the person mentioned most. He had played the role before, in a touring company a dozen years earlier. Nadine Thomas, who majored in theater arts in college and had some television work to her credit, was the person people thought should play Emily. A little makeup would take years off both of them.

Dutch had been in town only a day and a night. He hadn't shown up at the theater yet. Lionel phoned to brief Dutch on the candidates. He recommended Nadine and Simon.

"I've got my man already," Dutch said.

Lionel collected himself. "Really? Who?" he asked.

"Rudy Wheeler," Dutch answered.

A longer pause this time. "Rudy Wheeler," Lionel repeated. "Rudy Wheeler playing the Stage Manager?"

The only thing Lionel knew about Rudy was that he rented property for a living.

"I was listening to him describe Jeffrey to someone at the bar at the inn last night."

"I see," Lionel said. He didn't, of course. "Has he done anything before?"

"Not with his clothes on."

The pause was the longest yet. "I don't understand," Lionel said.

"A photographer took some nude pictures of him a couple of years ago."

"I had no idea," Lionel said, his tone of voice as close as he dared come to expressing his lack of enthusiasm from Dutch's decision.

Dutch had been drinking at the bar when he overheard Rudy, whose name he didn't know yet, describing Jeffrey to someone who was interested in a summer rental. It wasn't the sort of description Dutch expected. No boosterism at all. No talk of climate or amenities or attractions. Instead, a meditation on change, on differences, on past and present. Dutch could hear the man at the bar saying the Stage Manager's line "The morning star always sets wonderful bright the minute before it has to go," could hear him speaking those words with no dramatics, no false profundity, but with the perfect undertone of wistfulness. This man (people call me Rudy, he said when the client had left and Dutch introduced himself) was full of wistfulness.

"Be you," Dutch said whenever Rudy asked for advice during weeks of rehearsals.

There were four evening performances and two matinees. All to packed houses. Good reviews in the *Monitor* and *Union Leader,* papers that cover the state. The reviewers singled out Rudy for praise. In a letter, Simon DeWitt confessed to Rudy his surprise and disappointment with Dutch's choice, then congratulated Rudy on striking the right tone and giving a gratifying performance. Hats off to you, Simon wrote.

"You surprised me," Jimmy said. He placed Rudy's Johnny Walker on a cocktail napkin on the bar.

"I surprised myself," Rudy said.

"Much fan mail?"

"More voice mails and e-mails than I can answer, all about business. I should have hired a temp to tend the office."

Jimmy handed Rudy an envelope. "From one of your favorite clients," Jimmy said.

The paper gave off the scent of peonies. "Wynn?" Rudy asked. "Wynn was here?"

"'Passing through,' she said."

The drama itself was quite what I thought it would be, but you, Rudy, made it worth my evening. I hope I may give pleasure to one of yours. Wynn.

Rudy handed the letter to Jimmy. They hadn't noticed Dutch.

"From an admirer?" Dutch asked.

"His only fan letter," Jimmy said.

"Actually I got one from Simon DeWitt."

"Good to have choices," Dutch said. He ordered a martini.

"Are you expecting California company this summer?" Jimmy asked.

"This is a working summer," Dutch said.

"I thought the one with you last summer was work."

Dutch raised his glass. "Nice work if you can get it."

"And you could."

"For an almost-fifty guy, I do all right."

"Maybe you should invite Rudy to California and give him some pointers. He strikes out on a regular basis."

Dutch finished his martini. He left money on the bar to pay for his drink and Rudy's, with a large tip for Jimmy.

"Too much," Jimmy said.

"It's not for the service," Dutch said. "It's for the idea you just gave me."

Dutch sightings this year have been different. He's been regularly seen working in the college library, in the room that houses some of the town's archives. He's been reported to take long walks by himself, appearing deep in thought. He showed up at the inn for supper with different women. Twice with Anne Haber. ("Work I can't get.") Once with Marjorie Wheatley, who is ninety-five years old, and who borrowed a scarf from her granddaughter so she could ride to the inn in Dutch's convertible without asking him to put up the top. Jimmy reported she enjoyed two Dubonnets and a brandy. Dutch told no one that she fell asleep on the way home. Nor that he kissed her cheek before he woke her. Finally, a long dinner with Nadine Thomas, who phoned to make the reservation herself. She met the twenty-year-difference rule that applied to the California blondes. Nadine is blond too. Afterward in the bar Dutch drank port and Nadine nursed a wine. Jimmy had the impression that Dutch was trying to put himself to sleep and she was trying to stay awake. ("Work I don't want to get.")

In August, Dutch bought Rudy dinner. Dutch had with him a folder of photocopies, including one of his mother's picture in *Life*, as well as sketches and some pages of a script. "Beautiful," he said. "Refugees right here. The ones worst off lived with families. The older ones and the stronger ones stayed in cabins on the lake." Dutch spread out his photocopies of the refugee children and cabins he'd made from pictures in the archives. Rudy remembered the cabins. They'd belonged to a summer camp that went out of business.

The cabins were falling down in the seventies, when Rudy was growing up. Kids snuck into them to make out and smoke. Rudy's father-in-law had owned the property once. He tore down the cabins. A million-dollar house occupied the land now.

"Mrs. Wheatley remembers a refugee staying with her family. She's fuzzy about details. Anne Haber has some stuff from her family. There's enough in the archives to fill things out. I've started to write. Lots of voices. The refugees. The people in town. The narrator. He's sad no one remembers what happened here, how so many lives were changed. How this history has been forgotten. That's you, Rudy. That's you."

Dutch wouldn't have a script ready for at least a year, probably longer. He'd hire other writers to help him. But he wanted to show what he done so far to some television people. Dutch wanted Rudy to fly out to California and record the monologue he had written for him.

"You have a pleasing voice for commercials, by the way," Dutch said. "You might get some work. Both kinds," he said, and wiggled his eyebrows in a Groucho Marx kind of way.

There was a lull in rental business in early September. Rudy thought he might go then. He wasn't sure. He didn't like to travel. When he got to L.A. what would he do? He couldn't hang around Dutch all the time. He didn't know what Dutch would be like in his own space.

At least once a week Rudy read Wynn's note. Sometimes he thought she was promising she would see him again; sometimes he thought she was making a promise in the event they did meet again. He kept remembering their dinners together. Her clothes. Her body. The way she asked him questions. The answers she had in mind already. He missed her very much. He had never expected to see her again. But her note was in his hand. She had seen him even if he had not seen her. She was promising . . . Rudy couldn't decide.

Yes, he told Dutch. Yes, he would fly to California. An envelope from Dutch's production company arrived. Dutch had arranged for a jitney service to drive Rudy to Boston on Monday afternoon. He had a reservation at the Ritz. His flight to L.A. left early Tuesday morning. Enclosed was a first-class ticket on American Airlines.

Rudy checked in at the Ritz at five o'clock. He lay down and read the ads in the real estate section of the *Globe*. He tried to nap but couldn't. He took a walk on Newbury Street, then along Commonwealth, watching the windows begin to darken. Time for a Johnny Walker, he decided.

A waiter in a starched white jacket brought Rudy's drink, along with a small bowl of nuts and pretzels. Rudy thought the piano player was doing "Moon over Miami." Rudy hadn't heard it in a long time. He tried to name songs about Los Angeles.

"I knew I'd find you here," the voice behind him said.

Her dress was silk, ivory in color, with a matching unbuttoned jacket. She wore the jade ring Rudy remembered. Her lips were brushed a pale pink. A necklace of smooth dark beads matched her eyes.

"Wynn . . ."

"May I join you, Rudy?"

He stood up and pulled out a chair.

"I . . ."

She held up her hand. "No exclamations of surprise, Rudy. We don't need them."

He stared at her. Which he had done before, when he was sure she was reading his mind. She spoke her order, "A Sazerac, please," to the waiter without turning her face from Rudy's gaze. "They expect me to order what they consider exotic cocktails. I don't let them down," she said to Rudy when the waiter returned to the bar.

"Do you know Dutch Donovan or someone who works for him?" Rudy asked. Wynn shook her head. "Did someone in Jeffrey tell you?" She shook her head again. "How did you know?"

"It's that logic with you, isn't it? All must be explained. So Western."

"You can't have just shown up."

The Sazerac showed up. Wynn took a sip.

"You're right. I can't, and I didn't."

They drank their drinks, listened to the piano player, looked at each other, and ordered another drink.

"Do you like my dress, Rudy?"

"I've liked all your clothes."

"You complained once about the clothes I wore into the woods."

"No complaints now."

"I have one. I misjudged. I thought the season would be cooler."

"You have no idea how beautiful I think you are in that dress."

"Perhaps I do, Rudy. I think you will think I am beautiful too when I take it off," Wynn said.

She did not say, Rudy, you have no idea how surprised you look, although she considered saying so.

"I am prepared to go upstairs whenever you are," she said.

When they woke, they were hungry. Wynn phoned room service and asked for escargots, an endive salad, and a Chablis Rudy had never heard of. He ordered a shrimp cocktail and a tenderloin. "If your lovemaking were as predictable as your food ordering, I would have no wish to make love again," Wynn said.

In the morning the plop of a newspaper outside the door awakened Rudy. Time to shower and go to the airport. "Rudy," Wynn said, "there will be other planes."

Later he showered and dressed. "Rudy, have breakfast and bring me tea when you come back," Wynn said.

Downstairs, the waiters seemed distracted. Rudy ate quickly and returned to the room with Wynn's tea.

"Of course she was gone," Rudy said.

Jimmy had seen the light in Rudy's office. The inn had closed early. It was nine o'clock on Tuesday night.

"I phoned the airline for another flight. That's when I found out. I rented a car and drove home."

"I really thought you were dead."

"I should be.

"Just gone," Jimmy said.

"Just gone," Rudy said.

By the end of the week a dozen people had phoned Rudy and canceled their October reservations. The hardware store sold out of American flags and decals and ordered more.

Up Main Street they came, Rudy, with a woman wearing a head scarf, and a child. Most people in Jeffrey had seen Muslims only in pictures. They're visiting from Connecticut, Rudy said.

The woman's nephew worked in the kitchen at the inn. The family came from Iran. The nephew wore American clothes. He didn't live in town. No one paid any attention to him. The child's father was being detained, though an immigration lawyer assured the woman that her husband's documents were in order and he would be released eventually. People on the street in Hartford threatened the woman. She was afraid to leave her apartment. You will be safe here, her nephew told her. The inn had many empty rooms, so the woman, whose name is Waltaz Razavi, and her child were able to stay there. The gift shop down the street hired Mrs. Razavi to work part time.

On the way home from Boston, Rudy had phoned Dutch. We'll talk later, Dutch said. Now Dutch called to tell Rudy another project took priority and theirs would be on hold for a while. That was okay with Rudy. He thought about mentioning the woman and her child. In their way, they were refugees too. But he didn't. They needed privacy.

One day in Vivaldi's a man with a loud voice asked Mrs. Razavi why she was here. He meant why was she in Jeffrey? Mrs. Razavi thought he meant why was she in America. She answered, Because I have the dream you have forgotten. The man neither expected her to understand him nor to answer, especially in English he could understand. The man pushed his cart quickly up the aisle toward the free doughnuts and coffee. Priscilla Darrow, who had written the new, much admired town history, saw what happened, apologized, and offered Mrs. Razavi a ride home.

They drove through a bright autumn morning. When Mrs. Razavi got out of the car, Priscilla apologized again for the man in the market. "Most people in town want to welcome you," she said.

That night the topic among the regulars at the bar was Bill Appling. Bill managed money, his own, which was considerable, and other people's. His lottery ticket, the only one he ever bought, had just won him 100,000 more dollars.

"Luck or whatever. Can you believe it?" someone said.

Jimmy and Rudy exchanged glances. Whatever the *whatever* was Rudy believed it. He put his head down and smiled.